I0594309

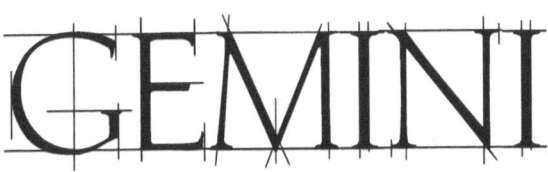

GEMINI

EDITED BY AUSTIN P. SHEEHAN,
NIKKY LEE & MATTHEW P. COPPING

THE ZODIAC SERIES

The Zodiac Series is a collection of twelve speculative fiction anthologies, each focusing on one of the Zodiac signs. The anthologies feature short stories and poems inspired by each sign, and retellings of the various myths behind those signs.

#

Capricorn Aquarius Pisces

Aries Taurus Gemini

Cancer Leo Virgo

Libra Scorpio Sagittarius

#

The Zodiac Series has been produced by Aussie Speculative Fiction, and each anthology contains a diverse selection of tales by talented writers from Australia and New Zealand.

First published by Deadset Press in 2020.

© Deadset Press 2020

Cover design Copyright © Alanah Andrews.

Edited by Austin P. Sheehan, Nikky Lee and Matthew P. Copping.

Foreword by Sasha Hanton.

I AM GEMINI

Zoey Xolton

I am the Twins and my constellation is Gemini.

My tarot card is The Lovers; I am a strong communicator and an artistic spirit.

At my best I am affectionate, curious and adaptable.

At my worst I am nervous, indecisive and inconsistent.

Intellectual and free, like my element: Air, mine is a Mutable sign.

I appreciate books, music, writing and stimulating conversation.

However, I dislike isolation, repetition and routine.

I am ruled by Mercury, and am guardian to the third day of the week.

My colours are green and yellow.

About the Author:

Zoey Xolton is an Australian Speculative Fiction writer, primarily of Dark Fantasy, Paranormal Romance, and Horror. Her works have appeared in over one-hundred themed anthologies, with more due for publication!

She has recently celebrated the release of her debut short story collection 'Darkly Ever After'. *You can find further details regarding her many publications on her website:* www.zoeyxolton.com*!*

CONTENTS:

FOREWORD

Sasha Hanton

One of the harder zodiac signs to pin down, Gemini bears a sense of duality. Represented by a set of twins, the third sign of the zodiac is sometimes referred to as two-faced and at other times loyal. As the mutable air sign, Gemini is open to changing when needed and can adapt to most situations.

The most notable myth surrounding Gemini focuses on the twins Castor and Pollux. These prominent characters of Greek mythology are also known as the Dioscuri, and while some aspects of their myths do not vary, many do.

Born from Leda, wife of Tyndareus, the King of Sparta, the Dioscuri are brothers of Helen (of Troy) and Clytemnestra. As Leda was also a lover of Zeus'—willing or unwilling depends on the variation of the myth, but all agree he "seduced" her whilst in the form of a swan—the major variation of the Dioscuri myth is in regards to their mortality.

Whilst some sources can't agree if they were born from an egg alongside their twin sisters, most do agree that the twins were half-brothers. As it goes, Castor was the son of Tyndareus and thus born mortal, whilst Pollux was a demigod sired by Zeus. In some variations both of the twins are depicted as mortal, which again changes other aspects of the story. Their myth is a rather long one, but the short version is that during a fight against their cousins the Leucippides, Castor is fatally wounded. In variations of the telling where Pollux is a demigod, Zeus offers him the option to spend the rest of his days on Mount Olympus, or to share half of his immortality with his brother. Unable to bear living without his brother, Pollux chooses the latter. And in those variations where Pollux is mortal, he sacrifices his life. In either variation, the result is the same. Zeus places their images among the stars, though in the version where Pollux is a demigod, this allows the Dioscuri to travel back and forth between Hades, the underworld, and Mount Olympus.

As with every zodiac sign, Gemini holds a close connection to one of the Major Arcana of the Tarot. Just as the mythology assigned to Gemini involves twins, the tarot card representative for Gemini features two intrinsically connected individuals, the Lovers. With all things regarding Gemini there is a sense of duality, and at the heart of it, that is what the Lovers card represents—two parts of a greater whole. The card depicts Adam and Eve, with Adam's gaze cast downwards and Eve's cast upwards, as they stand in front of the Tree of Life and the Tree of Knowledge respectively. Above them is an angel with its arms extended, and winding its way around the Tree of Knowledge is a serpent.

There are many interpretations for the symbolism of the Lovers, but it all comes back to duality and choice; the man can represent the conscious mind and the woman the subconscious, sacred love and

2

profane love, inner and outer life, good and evil. While not twins per se, the Lovers represent two different sides of the same person. It is a card invoking the power of choice, something that is of the utmost importance to Gemini.

Gemini individuals tend to be labelled as indecisive or flaky, but there is more to this sign. Most Geminis can see both sides of an argument; they are less indecisive than what others claim them to be. They are flexible and prone to change their mind. Governed over by the planet of Mercury, named for the Roman counterpart of the Greek God Hermes, Geminis are mercurial. The messenger god, from whom their ruling planet takes its name, is the god of communication, knowledge and curiosity—not to mention a whole slew of other responsibilities, which may perhaps explain why Gemini's so rarely fit a simple mould. These traits are passed on to those born between May 21st and June 20th in spades.

People are often quick to judge a Gemini, not looking past the first encounter to meet their other half. In this anthology, you'll see that duality is at the core of Gemini and you won't want to stop reading until you've uncovered all this tricky sign's secrets.

About the Author:

Sasha Hanton grew up in the tropics of Darwin, Northern Territory. From a young age, she devoured books and iced coffee, both of which she continues to intake on an almost daily basis. Now living on beautiful Bribie Island in Queensland, her time is split between writing and spoiling her puppy Miley.

Sasha, who has a Bachelor of Journalism from Bond University, has dabbled in the journalistic profession but finds fiction far more fascinating. Her first published work The Short Story Press Collection *draws on her love for a diverse range of genres and passion for short stories. Coming from a multicultural background (Eurasian) she aspires to make her writing inclusive for people from all walks of life and to bring a unique blend of eastern and western culture to her writing.*

Throughout her life, she has been a lover of history and mythology, and at any time will find some way to worm one or the other into her storytelling. When she's not writing or reading she can be found walking her dog and volunteering. You can keep up with her writing over on www.theshortstorypress.wordpress.com

WELCOME HOME

Belinda Brady

My twin sister, Freya, is waiting for me in the hallway as I enter our home. Her face is one of shock as she grabs me by the shoulders and moves in close. "Whatever you do," she whispers in my ear, her voice panicked, "don't let him know you know. As far as you're concerned, it's really him."

"Who?" I whisper back, confused.

Before she can answer, he appears behind her.

I pull back from my sister and inhale sharply. It takes all my strength to stay standing, to smile back at him, when all I want to do is turn and run.

"Welcome home, Alice! We've missed you!" Dad beams at me.

Freya is gaping at me, her eyes reflecting the horror I feel. I stare back at her, forcing my face to stay neutral.

My gaze shifts back to my father. The same father who raised us alone for ten years after our mother walked out when we were just eight years old. The same father who read us bedtime stories, taught us how to drive and was our shoulder to cry on when we experienced our first heartbreak. The same father who is now coming towards me with huge smile on his face, his arms outstretched for a hug.

The same father we buried over a year ago after he was killed in a car accident.

"Dad," I finally manage, as he wraps his arms around me. "It's so good to see you. I've missed you too."

He's exactly the same: he smells the same; he feels the same; he hugs the same. But it's not him. I know it.

"I've missed you so much, Alice. You and your sister." He smiles, his fingers gripping my forearms as we pull away from our embrace.

"It's been a while . . ." I look over to Freya, who remains glued to her spot.

"And that's why I'm here!" Dad exclaims. "To be with my girls, to be with my beautiful twins."

"Well, I'm really glad you're here." I smile back, my heart racing.

"I'm making us our favourite dinner—a roast with all the trimmings. I'm sure you can smell it. My famous gravy is simmering away on the stove and I'd hate to burn it, so come, follow me to the kitchen." He drops my arms and looks from my sister to me, grinning at us both.

"C'mon girls, don't just stand there. Your feast is waiting for you," he repeats and it's then that I see it—a flash. A blink-and-you'd-miss-it flash that fills his eyes with the purest of black. Every hair on my body stands on end.

"Oops! Nearly forgot!" he exclaims suddenly, his eyes widening. He barges between Freya and I, marches to the front door, and locks it with a key that has magically appeared in his hand. "I have Freya's key. I'll have yours now." He turns to me, hand outstretched.

Freya bows her head in silence. I open my mouth to ask why he has locked the front door, when he narrows his eyes at me.

"Now, Alice," he demands.

I bite my lip and hand him my key.

He places the two of them in the top pocket of his shirt, patting them in place. "Just to be safe. We don't want anyone interrupting out little reunion." He winks before he turns and walks down the hallway toward the kitchen.

Freya is by my side in an instant, grabbing my hand. "Did you see that?" she asks, her voice quivering.

"I did." I nod, trying to keep composed. If I lose it, she'll lose it, and that can't happen. To get out of this house, we need to keep it together. *I* need to keep it together. "Tell me everything from the beginning."

"I came home from school early, my science teacher was sick or something so our class was cancelled and there he was in the kitchen, cooking dinner. I nearly died from shock. He told me he missed us, he wanted to see us again, so he thought he'd drop in, cook us a meal just like he used to," Freya blurts out, her eyes darting to the hallway. "I know it's not him, I *know* it. I was so afraid of what to do, what to say, so I just went along with it. He was talking like nothing had happened—asking how school was, asking when you were getting home. I tried to get to the front door to get out, but he was in front of me in a flash, blocking my way, wanting to know what I was doing, demanding my house key . . . Jesus, Alice. What the hell is going on?"

7

"I don't know," I answer, "but one thing is certain. Whoever that is, it's not our Dad. We need to stick together on this. Don't let on we know, don't show him we know. We just need to keep our cool until we can work out how to get out of here."

Freya nods, tears spilling from her glassy eyes.

I pull her into a hug. "Just follow my lead. We're going to get out of this, okay?"

Dad sticks his head around the corner. "Are you girls coming? I can't wait for you to see what I've got prepared for you!"

"We're coming," I reply, releasing my sister from my arms, forcing a smile as he looks at me expectantly. "And we can't wait to see what you've got for us."

We walk into the kitchen to find it bustling with activity. Saucepans are bubbling noisily on the stove. The oven is on, our dinner cooking, emitting warmth and delicious aromas. My father returns to the stove stirring his gravy. I stand in the entrance and stare at the scene before me, not sure what to do next.

"I know how much you two enjoyed my roasts, so I thought I'd whip one up for you. A welcome home meal if you like. A welcome home meal for my girls and I . . . my beautiful twins," he says, keeping his back turned as he stirs. "My girls who couldn't be any more different if they tried. Isn't that right, Freya?"

He turns to look at Freya, who is leaning against the bench near the sink, nodding her head in a zombie-like trance. "Well, Freya? Cat got your tongue? Speak!" he snaps, his tone taking a dark turn.

WELCOME HOME

"Sorry . . . yes, we are different, Alice and I. Typical twins, typical Geminis. I'm the impulsive, superficial, emotionally detached one, while sis here is the intelligent, outgoing, yet more anxious, twin. I tend to do things without thinking, while she is frustratingly indecisive and takes forever to make a decision. It takes her a week to decide what she wants for lunch." Freya laughs, a sudden and unexpected confidence to her voice.

Dad smiles at Freya and something passes between them—a look, a knowing look.

My breath catches in my throat and my stomach drops as I realise my sister knows something I don't. Dread crawls up my chest as Dad turns back to the stove and Freya stays by the bench, staring at the back of him. She won't make eye contact with me. I fight to keep my breathing steady as my mind races, trying to think of a way to make it out of this house safely and away from them both.

"Oh damn it!" the man who looks like my father exclaims, turning around with an empty salt bottle in his hands. "I'm out of salt, and this gravy is nothing without it. Do you reckon there's some in the back shed?"

"I'll go look!" I offer, jumping at my chance to flee. I turn and make a beeline for the back door, fighting the urge to run as I make my way through the back of the house. Reaching the door, I turn the knob and pull it open with a violent yank, as though my life depends on it.

Because it does.

Stale afternoon air hits my face as I exit the house and make my way to the shed, still not running, but not far off it. The shed is home to a variety of weird and wonderful tools—it's also where we store any

9

excess groceries. It stands just behind the house, separated by a small footpath, its only door facing our huge backyard. Opposite it, built into the fence, is a gate that leads to a back laneway—and my escape. The shed door is a noisy, creaky thing and there's no mistaking the sound when it's being opened. I know they'll be waiting for that creak of the door; the flicker of the light as it's switched on. I have to go inside for just a second, make them think I'm looking for the salt, when I've really snuck through the gate to my freedom. It's risky, but it's my only chance. I have to get out. I *have* to try . . .

Hands shaking, I open the door and wait for the dust to clear before I step inside, swatting away a few flies that buzz past my face. I turn on the light and scream.

In the corner, propped up like a doll, is the body of Freya. It is bloated and pasty, dried vomit crusted to the side of her face and down her neck, her dead eyes staring back at me in silence. Lying next to her is the body of my father, which I had not seen since his funeral. He was broken and bruised then, and still is now, only decomposition had well and truly taken over. I fight the urge to vomit as maggots and flies crawled in and out of his mouth. Before them lies an altar, a pentagram filled with black candles, glass jars filled to the brim with items of various sizes and colours, and several family photos of the three of us, smiling happily for the camera. I turn to run, but Freya and my father are behind me, blocking the doorway. Their skin is pale, almost translucent, their eyes jet black, the same happy smiles from the family photos plastered across their faces.

"What? What happened . . . I don't . . ." I gasp as I grab the wall for support, my legs threatening to collapse at any moment.

WELCOME HOME

"You know I wasn't coping with the death of Dad," Freya starts, her voice higher than usual. "We lost him too soon, too young. It was so unfair."

Dad nods in response, his eyes on me, his face giving nothing away.

"I just couldn't get over it. I couldn't. I was so grief-stricken that I didn't see the point of carrying on, so I contemplated ending it all. But then I had a thought— 'what if I can get him back and things can go back to how they were before he died?'" Freya takes a step toward me. "So after a bit of searching on the dark web, I found a way. I found a spell. Not one that could bring back the dead, but one that could return things to how they were . . . before. It was one that can transport you back to that life before death, before loss. We could have our old lives back, the only catch being at least two of the parties involved in the spell couldn't be alive for it to work, we *had* to be dead, which was fine by me. I mean, Dad was already taken care of, so all I had to do was take care of myself, right? Then we could live our lives again. Not as spirits per se, but as the dead living their old lives in a perfect, unbreakable bubble. To the outside world, we didn't exist and never did. Our lives and memories would be completely wiped and we could just live our lives as they were without interruption. It was exactly what I wanted."

It's at that moment I notice the weather. *Really* notice it. It's June, our birthday month, the beginning of winter, and the air should be brisk and cold, but all I can feel, all I can smell, is warm air and fresh cut grass. Looking past them to the backyard, I see the trees are in full bloom, their foliage an explosion of green. The sun is high in the late afternoon sky, and a pair of swimmers are on the clothesline, dripping water on the grass below as they dry, fresh from a swim at the beach. A typical summer's day.

"What's the date?" I stutter, already knowing the answer.

"It's the twentieth of January," my dad replies solemnly.

The day he died.

"The day he died," Freya states, reading my mind. "I'm sure you remember, Alice. You had just come home from the beach and Dad was cooking dinner, his famous roast, when he was called into work. An elevator had malfunctioned at the local shopping centre and he had to go and repair it. Dad promised he'd be back in time to make his gravy, but never did. He was involved in an accident, a head-on collision, and died instantly. That was the day it all turned to shit."

"I was just as upset about dying as you and Freya were, Alice," Dad continues, moving next to Freya, "I had such *anger* attached to my death, but lucky for us—*all* of us—your sister here found a way to get us all back to that afternoon before I was killed, before I left for work. She found a way to get us back to that life, that safe, happy life and now it will be our new existence. It will be our *only* existence."

"My god, Freya, what have you done?" I murmur, hot tears wetting my cheeks.

"It took me a while to get what I needed, of course," Freya continues, ignoring my question. "Some things were super hard to come by, such as goat embryos and cow's blood, but I got them, and I got them past you. Remember all those parcels that were being delivered? The ones I told you were clothes I'd bought on sale?"

I nod slightly, remembering the influx of plain packaged parcels Freya had been getting almost daily a few weeks back. She had told me her favourite online clothing store was having a 'huge, once-in-a-lifetime sale', when I questioned her spending and naively didn't think to push it.

She turns her head and looks at Dad, a satisfied smirk on her face. "But where there's a will there's a way, and I got every damn item the spell required. I knew you'd never go for it, you and your anxious little mind, so I kept it to myself. After all, I didn't want to spoil the surprise."

She inches closer, Dad right behind her.

"I dug Dad up that weekend you went away with your friends, stashed him away in here. Boy, what an effort that was. I had to wait till after midnight to go to the cemetery, dig him up, lug his heavy body back to the car and then fix up his grave. The cemetery never noticed of course—I made sure his grave was in pristine condition when I left. But it had to be done—he was a pivotal part of the magic. I needed to end my life right after I cast the spell, but I had no objections. If it worked, bonus, if not . . . bonus. The overdose was messier than I had anticipated. Funny that." She looks over my shoulder to her vomit-soaked body and laughs. "But it was worth it. We are back here, back to this day, back to this moment before Dad leaves the house. We are back to that moment when he is here; preparing dinner and everything is just so freaking perfect. We just need to finish the spell now and this will be how it is forever—Dad and his twin girls living this day, living this life on repeat."

Freya's face hardens as her black eyes meet mine, her arms moving to the front of her body, revealing a hammer in her curled hand. "It's time to finish the spell, Alice."

Dad lunges from the doorway and is behind me before I can blink. He grabs at my arms, trying to hold them against my sides, but

I break free, pushing him away as I make a desperate dash for the door. I charge at Freya, knocking her to the floor, her screams muffled as the blood rushes in my ears and I burst into our backyard. My adrenaline is pumping as I run, gasping for air, grass crunching under my feet, as the gate to the laneway gets closer.

There's movement and shouting behind me and everything slows down. I'm still running but I'm moving in slow motion, the gate sliding away from me, as though imaginary strings are pulling it back.

I hear a whooshing sound and turn to see the hammer coming straight for me, flying through the air with a guided grace. Freya is in front of the shed, her left arm mid-pitch, her face twisted in rage as she chants words I don't understand. Dad is next to her, arms crossed, his face creased into an impatient scowl. The hammer connects with my temple, the sound of cracking bone loud and sickening, the pain instant and breathtaking. I hear laughter; the loud and hysterical laughter of my sister as I collapse in a heap, blood gushing from my broken skull, soaking the grass underneath me as my life slips away. The last thing I hear before I take my last breath, before I join my dead family in their unearthly new world, is Freya's singsong voice calling out from the circling darkness.

"Welcome home, Alice."

About the Author:

Belinda is passionate about stories and after years of procrastinating, has finally turned her hand to writing them, with a preference for supernatural and thriller themes; her love of both often competing for her attention. She has had several stories published in print, online and in anthologies, in a variety of publications. Belinda lives in Australia with her family, and has been known to enjoy the company of cats over people.

Belinda's story, 'Break the Spell' *was published in Aussie Speculative Fiction's anthology,* 'Beginnings'.

Adam's Imaginary Friend

Carolyn Young

Lots of kids have imaginary friends, but Adam didn't know anyone who had one like his. Everyone else he knew played with their friend; they had fun together. Adam didn't play with his, and he wasn't around all the time. He couldn't summon him whenever he wanted, and he couldn't stop him from showing up when he'd rather be alone. And most of the time, he'd rather be left alone, because Adam's imaginary friend scared him.

Adam couldn't remember a time before Derek became his friend. His mum often told him how cute he used to be as a toddler, sitting on the shag-pile carpet in his room and zooming his cars around a track while giggling for Derek to drive faster. She used to say how much happier he was when they were playing together. But all Adam could recollect was the pain and fear.

For as long as he could remember, Derek visited him in his dreams. He was often woken by a racing heart, tangled in sheets and wet with perspiration—or sometimes, he hated to admit, with urine. Even after he was much too old to wet the bed.

Awakening from the nightmares should have been the end of the terror, but after waking, he knew to expect the pain—and the screams so loud in his head he could barely think. He'd lie there paralysed with fear, unable to move or utter even the smallest cry for help waiting for the onslaught to end. Powerless to stop the pain or to understand its source, he'd lie there with tears dripping from his cheeks, battered to the point where he expected to die. But upon waking the next morning, he could never seem to find a mark on his body.

Once, when he was still small, he went through a time he thought of as the "hungry time". No amount of food would fill his grumbling stomach. He couldn't concentrate on anything else but his feelings of hunger, no matter how much he'd eaten. His mother had asked him why he was so hungry, but she just smiled at him when he said it wasn't him who was hungry; it was Derek. She added an extra chair to the table and set a place for Derek from then on.

Adam wanted to scream at her and tell her that wasn't how it worked. But she just told him not to be embarrassed; lots of kids his age had imaginary friends and when he was older, he wouldn't need Derek anymore, and he'd go away.

But Derek didn't go away.

As Adam got older, the nightmares came and went, but a few days after his twelfth birthday, Adam woke up screaming in pain. He was so loud his parents ran into the room, thinking someone had broken in. Adam fought to breathe through the terror of feeling like something was crushing his body. An ambulance was called, and he was taken to hospital.

The hospital ran tests, but the doctors found no reason for his pain, or his struggle to breathe. He spent weeks in the hospital, hooked up to bags that pumped in painkillers and made it hard to think straight. It took months to regain enough strength and coordination to walk again. Years later, his right arm would still become weak and ache sometimes.

He tried to talk to his mum about it, but she just shrugged and said, "It's just one of those things. We don't know what caused the pain or why, but you just need to accept that your arm doesn't work as well as it did before and get on with your life."

"Mum, maybe it was something to do with Derek," Adam said quietly, voicing an idea that had haunted him during his months of recovery.

"Not Derek again. It used to be cute, but most kids grow out of their imaginary friends by the time they're seven or eight. You need to get over this nonsense."

He never mentioned Derek to her again, but that didn't mean he went away. The nightmares continued, but instead of pain and fear, Adam was overcome by rage, violence, and visions of blood.

Even as an adult—married and with children of his own—Adam still woke up a couple of nights each week, dripping wet and traumatised. Hours after Leonie had helped him change the sheets and pulled him into her arms, he still trembled with fear. She had been the first to suggest he talk to a doctor, and after returning home with a course of sleeping tablets, he was able to sleep peacefully for a while.

An unexpected call changed all that when Adam was thirty-five. His parents had died in a car accident a few months earlier and the call had come from a lawyer entrusted with the distribution of their estate.

"Adam, I'd like to organise a time to meet with you to pass on a few personal items that your parents wanted you to have after they passed," she'd said.

They'd scheduled a time for later in the week; the first hint of what lay ahead was when she asked if he could bring someone with him to the appointment for support.

Sitting next to Leonie in the waiting room, Adam's heart raced, and his legs trembled. He couldn't explain it, but he felt like what he would to hear would change his life forever.

"Your parents had a secret that they kept from you but wanted you to know after they had passed," the lawyer began. "These are the documents they asked me to give you."

Adam reached out, his hands damp with perspiration. Adoption papers from the Redburn Adoption Agency blurred before his eyes. "I was adopted?" he asked. "Why didn't they tell me?"

"Back in those days, most adoptions were kept from the kids. Your parents loved you, and they always planned on telling you, but the right time never came. Last time I saw them, they told me they felt it was too late to tell you themselves, but they wanted you to know in the event of their deaths."

The room spun as Adam tried to come to terms with the news. A mix of confusion and rage duelled within his body. *How could they have kept this from me?*

"What about my birth family?" he whispered, his voice hoarse with emotion.

"As per your parents' request, we did some research on your birth family and a report is in this envelope. I'm sorry to say, but both of your birth parents are deceased, but you do have one surviving sibling. An identical twin brother. His name is Derryn. No, wait. That's not right; let me check." The lawyer fumbled through some paperwork on her desk.

"Derek?" Adam asked, his face becoming paler as his heart raced.

"Yes. Derek. That's right. But how did you know?"

Adam leant forward, cradling his face in his trembling hands. "I guess I've always known deep down. So, how do I find him?"

Derek wasn't surprised when he received a call from his brother; he'd always known he was a twin. His mother would often remind him of how she'd chosen to keep him over Adam. She thought reminding him of how much she'd wanted to keep him would make him feel special. It would have, too, if his father's alcoholism hadn't overshadowed their lives.

Many nights Derek would lie in bed wishing he could swap places with the twin who had been sent away—the one who had a chance to live free from the constant threat of violence. Over the years he'd often caught glimpses of his brother's life through the bond they shared. He could tell Adam was loved and cared for.

He'd learned fairly early he had a bond with his twin brother. He used to imagine they were playing together when he was very small, but the first time he realised they could pass things between them was one day when he felt dizzy, then his knee stung. He could hear his brother crying and feel the comforting hug of Adam's brother. He could even picture the bicycle his brother had fallen off, complete with its wonky training wheel.

It hadn't taken him long to master the technique of sending his most intense emotions and discomforts to Adam. When his father woke him during the night to terrorise him, he just concentrated really hard and followed the bond that took him to Adam. He could stay there for as long as he wanted, returning only when the blows stopped and his father passed out on the floor. He knew all the pain and frustration he'd sent to his brother over the years, so it was with some trepidation he agreed to meet him.

The bond they'd shared had become weaker throughout the years. He no longer found it easy to push his negative emotions towards his brother. Or he hadn't until Adam had learned of his existence. Now, it was all too easy. All Derek had to do was think about Adam and he could hear his thoughts, feel his emotions, and experience first-hand his joy at learning he had a brother. He'd heard the argument Adam had with Leonie when she'd said she didn't want him to meet Derek on his own. He'd even felt the waves of pleasure Adam had that night when he'd made love to his wife.

Make-up sex—nothing was better than that, he thought and sighed. *How happy Adam seemed to be.*

Derek wondered, not for the first time, which one of them was really the "chosen" one—himself, who had been chosen to stay with his biological parents; or Adam, who'd had the chance to start a fresh life. Pangs of jealousy coursed through him.

Standing at the airport and waiting for Adam's plane to arrive, it was hard to tell whose emotions belonged to whom. The nervous racing heart he was sure belonged to Adam, the sweaty palms were his own. Despite knowing what Adam would look like, Derek was still taken by surprise when he saw his brother for the first time. Identical didn't describe it. They'd even dressed the same in their denim jeans, white t-shirts, and black windcheaters tied around their waists.

A grin erupted across his own face, mirrored by Adam as they threw themselves into a strong embrace. Derek pulled away first, his weak right arm annoying him, which had never fully healed after the car accident he'd been in when he was twelve.

Adam looked at his brother's scarred arm. "What happened to you?"

"I was in a car accident years ago. Dad was drunk, and he hit a tree. It's never been the same since."

"Wait," Adam said, massaging his own right arm. "When did this happen?"

"Just after my twelfth birthday. Dad said he'd take me out to celebrate, but he'd already started the celebration before he picked me up. The bastard nearly killed me. Broken bones in both legs, cracked ribs. You should see the rest of my scars. They had to piece me back together. I was in the hospital for months."

"Yeah, me too," Adam said quietly. "Did you know?"

"Know what?"

"That we had some sort of bond. That I could feel what you felt?"
Derek nodded.

"Why don't we go get a drink and catch up? There's so much I
want to know," Adam said.

They spent the next few hours exchanging stories of their lives and
talking about their parents. Derek discussed the "hungry time" when
his Dad was out of work for six months and they didn't have enough
to eat.

"How did they die?" Adam asked.

"Murder-suicide," Derek said, taking another gulp of his beer and
looking away.

"How long ago?"

"Oh, I dunno—a few years back. Really sent me off the rails for a
while. I was so pissed at my dad I took it out on everyone else."

"I remember that time. I could feel your anger, but I didn't
understand it, or know where it came from. You scared the life out of
me."

"Sorry, mate. Well, it's all in the past now. I eventually got my life
back on track."

"So, what happens now?" Adam asked.

"Why don't I show you around? Let you see the house I grew up
in, and I'll take you to where I scattered Mum and Dad's ashes if you
like."

"Thanks. I'd like that."

The house where Derek had grown up was small and run down. Dirt covered the windows, their frames lined with spiderwebs. The place reeked of abandonment, which Derek confirmed as true. He hadn't been able to sell it after his parents' death. They'd been found covered in blood, crumpled in the living room, with matching gunshot wounds to the head. The authorities had never found a suicide note, and the police still considered it an open case. No one wanted to buy the house. The locals said it was haunted.

Derek pulled a key from his pocket and slotted it into the front door. The rusted latch refused to budge before it gave a loud screech as Derek dislodged whatever had been stopping it. Reluctance shivered through Adam at the thought of entering the house where his biological parents had died. It felt wrong, like he would see their crumpled bodies and the blood still on the walls, but he followed Derek inside, not wanting to appear weak.

Derek switched on his torch. The house was dark and cold inside even though the sun hadn't fully set. Following closely behind, Adam scanned the kitchen, then followed Derek up the stairs to his old room. It looked vaguely familiar to him, but mostly he was overcome with sadness at the state of the room's neglect. Wallpaper had peeled from the walls, and the door hung at an angle with only a dirty, stained mattress laying in the corner as evidence anyone had ever lived there.

After quietly standing there for a few moments, Derek showed him their parents' room, then the small bathroom down the hallway covered in black mildew and dust blown in through the broken window.

Adam saw Derek take a deep breath as they descended the stairs to the living room. He sensed Derek's reluctance to enter the room and reached forward to stop him. "You don't have to go in there, if you don't want," Adam said.

"It's fine. It was a long time ago."

Entering the room, it was Adam who needed support though. The room was the same one from his nightmares—the same wallpaper, the same mirror over the fireplace. He could even remember the placement of the furniture that was no longer there: the dirty brown sofa that used to sit in the far corner; the lamp that once stood beside the television stand, the grubby cream carpet.

He couldn't see the carpet as it was now, or even how it had looked back then. He could only see it drenched in fresh blood and the smears of grey gore trailing down the leg of the coffee table. He remembered his worst nightmare—the one full of rage that had ended with blasts and an endless red sea of blood covering everything. He took a few unsteady steps backwards before his brother's arm reached out to stop his fall. He still remembered his parents' blood spattered over that scarred arm. He could even smell the burn of gunpowder.

He ran, stumbling through the front door, before losing his dinner all over the cracked path which lead to the street. His heart raced as Derek came up behind him, placing a hand on his shoulder—the same hand that had brutally killed their parents. Adam knew without a shadow of a doubt that he was next. It was well hidden, but he could feel the faint stirrings of jealous rage emanating from Derek.

Looking around wildly, he saw they were alone. Empty fields surrounded the house, the long heads of grass nodded at him as if confirming the danger he was in.

"Let me show you where I scattered their ashes, then I'll take you back to your hotel," Derek gripped Adam's shoulder like a vice.

"I'm not feeling well. Maybe I should go now, and we can see it tomorrow," Adam replied, his voice shaky.

"It won't take long. It's just over the road."

Seeing no other option, Adam cursed himself for not letting anyone know where he was going, and for not giving himself an escape route. He'd known from their bond that Derek was potentially dangerous. It was why he'd chosen to come by himself, leaving Leonie at home with the kids. But, he felt nothing from Derek now. If Derek meant to harm him, he'd know, he'd be able to feel it.

He followed Derek, searching for any escape route, anything he could use to defend himself if needed, but found nothing, just the bobbing heads of grass still nodding.

Standing at the edge of the cliff and overlooking the ocean, Adam surveyed the jagged rocks and high waves with trepidation. Everything in his body told him he was in danger, but he felt nothing through his bond with Derek. He trusted that bond; it hadn't ever let him down. He always knew when Derek was unstable, and he didn't feel it now.

"You scattered their ashes into the ocean? You chose a gorgeous spot," Adam said.

"I did," Derek replied, sighing. "It was somewhere that was special to our mother. I wanted her to spend eternity where she

27

would be happy. She always hoped she'd get to meet you again before she died . . ." he circled Adam, ". . . but since she didn't get the chance in life, I want to give her that chance in death."

An icy shiver ran through Adam's body. He turned in horror; looked into the cold eyes of his brother as the log of wood smashed the front of his skull.

Derek reached out with his mind to try to connect with his twin but sensed nothing. He couldn't feel anything from Adam, and when he tried to push his exhilaration towards him, he received no response. It had taken a lot of mental effort to block his intentions from his brother, but finally, their bond was broken.

He threw the blood-spattered log over the cliff, then rolled Adam's body off the edge. He turned away, not even waiting to hear the thud as it landed on the rocks below.

The following night, Leonie waited up for Adam to return from meeting Derek. She was surprised he hadn't called her as he'd promised. She'd had a bad feeling about the trip, but Adam had been keen to meet his brother and had insisted on going alone. She breathed a sigh of relief when she heard his car pull into the driveway and the fumbling of keys at the front door. Opening the door, she pulled him into her arms.

"I missed you. How did it go with Derek?"

"Let's just say I don't think we'll be seeing each other again."

"Do you want to talk about it?"

"Maybe later. I'm tired; can we go to bed?"

In reply, Leonie took his hand, smiled and led him to the bedroom. As she turned to switch on the bedside lamps, he stopped her.

"Leave them off," he said quietly, removing his shirt before pulling her into his arms.

Leonie reached up to kiss him before slipping her dress over her shoulders and climbing into bed beside him. As he reached for her, the streetlamp lit the scars on his arm and Leonie froze in terror. "Wait. Where did you get those scars?" she asked, as the weight of his naked body pressed on top of her own.

He smiled at her with a grin so evil she gasped. "I've had them for years," he whispered into her ear as his hand gripped her breast harder than he ever had. "You feel so good."

Leonie's screams rang across the neighbourhood before the sound of a single gunshot reverberated through the streets.

About the Author:

Carolyn Young is a single mum living in Melbourne with her children and rescue cats. Most of her writing falls under the speculative fiction banner with Young Adult dystopian as her main focus. She has several short stories appearing in both Australian and international publications.

A considerable amount of her life has been spent moving from one university course to another trying to find her place in the world before realising her interest in reading extended to an even stronger passion for writing.

She now spends her spare time reading, writing and dreaming of the day she can move to the country and write full-time.

As a writer she credits any and all success to her cat, who always knows the right keys to walk over to inspire creativity.

Carolyn's short story, 'The Beginning of the End' *was published in Aussie Speculative Fiction's anthology,* 'Beginnings.'

Follow Carolyn at
www.facebook.com/authorcarolynyoung.

THE CAT CRIES AT 3AM

Brianna Bullen

Déjà vu, you
feel it too?
In a dream of dual
cats, identical:

One sits by the windowsill
eyes glazed with bird static
from the sparrows in its own TV-
screen of reality made obscene.

Ignorance perched as its other walks
through the doorway. The image f/l/i/c/k/e/r/s
with an annoyed tail, yo-yo retractable.
Ears are erect to sound distorted—
a yowl of communion cleaves silence.

One sits by the windowsill

as its other balks: unfaithful mirror,
ornate trim. Glitches, before feline clockwork circuits
fire beneath the skin, moving
under its own gaze. Patchwork
tortoiseshell slowly shuffles over muscles.
A shifting mirage.

—Mechanically precise nature
meets Bastet biology—

We interpret markings
on bodies like clouds.
On the shoulder: an abstract grey Godzilla surrounded
by ginger flames, an old-school sailor tattoo
for the nuclear future
walking away
with feline flounce. We check its partner-rival.

For inconsistency: it inverts the colours, orange figure in
grey
fire overshadowed by smoke, whisper on the breeze.

Whiskers waver with worldly knowledge
into its own instability. It jumps onto the piano
and demands we play something by Yiruma. Conducting
from above, a streak of lightning feels
the vibrations between face and feet.
My sister takes the seat, back straight, baby-stepping
arpeggio.

THE CAT CRIES AT 3AM

Moggy scenting mahogany. Cheeks rubbing

at edges, sandpaper tongue

smoothing years off: enter childhood.

Fur Elise dancing in the dust motes of a lazy afternoon light.

Yet: it is midnight.

Paws pad staccato into peace. The dance: a dream

meaning nothing, curious only

for being shared

among siblings.

One sits by the windowsill

as its other

talks.

About the Author:

Brianna Bullen is a Deakin University PhD creative writing candidate writing about memory in science fiction. She has had work published in journals including LiNQ, Aurealis, Voiceworks, Rabbit, Multiverse: An International Anthology of Science Fiction Poetry, *and* Woolf Pack Zine.

She won the 2017 Apollo Bay short story competition and placed second in the 2017 Newcastle Short story competition. Her manuscript was previously a finalist in the 2018 Subbed In Poetry Chapbook competition. In 2018, she was part of Nexus, an Arts Access Victoria collective for artists with mental health recovery lived experience.

SAMSARA

Marcus Turner

I don't want to go in there, Alice thought, staring at the graffitied culvert entrance. The darkness yawned only a few metres beyond, giving the impression of a sudden dead-drop—a short walk to the back of a demon's throat.

A deep, constant growl rumbled from below. It was only the rush of subterranean waters, probably little more than a trickle magnified by the concrete tunnels. Still, unnerving. It seemed like a portent. The longer she stared into the tunnel, the less she wanted to go in, and it had little to do with Tommy. But there was no way around it. She was the only one that could find him.

Damn it, Tommy. What were you doing here?

The hangover wasn't helping anything. She'd called the office this morning, apologised and feigned a cough she was pretty sure the editor Russell didn't believe, but he'd given her a pass. Her feature wasn't due for another week anyway. He'd have been decidedly less impressed if he knew about the hangover, wondering if they were going to have another *blow-off.* She was committed to not falling off the wagon again, but all the same she'd polished off an entire bottle of vodka last night, trying to shut out the screams and pain.

Just like last time, the grog had only made things worse.

Taking a deep breath, Alice turned on her headlamp, tested her small backup torch before returning it to her pocket, and took that first terrifying step. The darkness welcomed her, drawing her into its frigid embrace. Traffic on the freeway above ebbed away as did the daylight. The sum of civilisation, reduced to its dank, foul-smelling guts.

Alice trudged, groaning, up a small flight of slippery steps, mini waterfalls of putrid water. Her shoes were already waterlogged, and the rubbing at her heel whispered of blisters by day's end. She tried not to think about the microbes and parasites in the water, the city's collective waste circling her feet. Why would anyone come down here willingly?

What if there are people living down here? The thought sent a chill across her skin. That was crazy. Who would want to live down in the tunnels? Who could bear the smell, the rats, the spiders?

Alice took her time along the stairs—the submerged steps were slick with slime, and the way the darkness swallowed her so completely, save for the narrow cone of light in front of her, compounded her spontaneous sense of claustrophobia. Her breath caught and a terrible throbbing, pulsing in time with the tenebrous darkness, beat like slave-galley drums in her ears. The certainty that something bad had happened to her twin only grew worse, an insidious whisper in her anxious mind.

Still . . . her intuitions when it came to Tommy were rarely wrong—if not by their connection then simply by knowing his character. And it went both ways. *The only friend a twin can rely on is its other half,* Tommy used to say.

Not used to, Alice admonished herself. *He's not dead. I'd know if he was.*

The tunnel soon ended in an overflow and a waterfall spilling out over a sheer wall-face. A twisted metal ladder dangled out at a precarious, oblique angle to the overflow, connected by a thick chain on the upper part of the frame and fixed to the wall on the lower. It was the only way up.

Alice tested the bottom rung with her foot. The frame shifted, but the chain held the ladder in place. She put her full weight on the ladder—the ladder suddenly toppled, her left foot slipping off the rung, and she cried out in alarm before the chain jerked taut. Alice paused, resisting the urge to leap off the ladder and double back. *Fuck this shit.* But after a few moments of composing herself, she continued her ascent. It was a twenty-foot climb, and at such an unnatural angle, her limbs began burning quickly.

She had almost reached the top when the shift in weight caused the ladder to tip forwards towards the waterfall. A short scream escaped her throat as the ladder crashed down on the concrete lip with a teeth-rattling clang. Her white-knuckle grip on the slimy rungs was the only thing that stopped her from being dislodged. That'd be a great way to go—breaking her back in a concrete pipe. Paralysed, slowly dying of starvation, or some bacterial infection from a broken bone or two sticking out of her flesh . . . if the rats or whatever else didn't eat her first, her corpse making a nice, rotting home for the earwigs and spiders.

Goddamnit, girl. Get a grip.

Alice climbed up the final rungs and onto solid ground. Another tunnel opened before her, changing into a coffin shape halfway down. Sloshing through the murky stream, she arrived in a spacious tunnel with high ceilings and humped banks on either side of the channel. Graffiti art and tags covered every inch of visible wall. Along the right-hand wall a large white grid had been spray-painted and filled with tags and signatures—a guestbook for urban explorers. Discarded beer bottles, pinwheels of cigarette butts and snack wrappers littered the space. *I can't believe people come down here for fun*, she thought.

Did Tommy come down here on a Cave Clan junket and get lost? Fall and injure himself, only to have his companions freak out and bail on him?

He was in pain—that much was certain. A shiver ran through her body that had nothing to do with the moist chill in the air.

Where are you?

The spacious chamber narrowed into a tight square passageway, and she was forced to trudge through more fetid water, hunching over to make it through. The air became staler and more pungent. The light refracted more brightly off the tight, compacted walls, but her claustrophobia only grew worse—she'd never shared such close quarters with so many redback and huntsman spiders before. The animal instinct to flee became more violent, reaching a hissing, spitting crescendo inside. But still she pressed on.

When the square tunnel eventually petered out into a larger space with fewer spiderwebs, Alice took a moment to consult her map. She was grateful she'd taken one explorer blogger's advice to draw it in permanent marker on a piece of white fabric—the cotton was already wet, but the markings were still legible. A paper map wouldn't have survived the journey this long. The tunnel went on straight for a while longer, before splitting off in two directions. One went on a winding route that supposedly led out to the river—the other delved deeper into the sewer network, becoming narrower and even more labyrinthine.

Hesitating, Alice closed her eyes, breathing slowly and steadily. *Darkness; the air smells foul. There's no water there.* As much as she dared hope to find her brother closer to the surface, just being a dick and partying with a bunch of sewer-dwelling losers, she knew him better than that. He wouldn't come here for that, and certainly not to hang out with *them.* He was *deep,* far deeper in the shit than either had realised or intended, literally and metaphorically speaking.

But that was the question: if not that, what the hell did he come down here to do?

She folded the map and put it back into her pocket. As she started to move again, a piece of graffiti above the portal caught her eye:

The end is not nigh. Then below it, by a less confident hand: *Time to head back!*

Great, Alice thought. *Thanks.*

Alice followed the pipe and soon emerged into another big chamber. The paths diverged at this point but—no, this was all wrong. She whipped the map back out, scanning it frantically.

No . . . no no no . . . Shit, this is wrong. I made a mistake somewhere!

39

The tunnel on her copied map branched off in only two directions. The tunnel she stood in split off four ways. *Fuck!* How could she have messed up so badly? She'd cross-referenced with original council maps, hand-drawn maps and detailed accounts on urban exploration blogs—she'd memorised most of the network's prominent features, but she did *not* remember a four-way junction. It's possible the council maps were outdated—she hadn't checked dates—and urban explorer cartography wasn't exactly a precise science.

Don't panic. The path to the right should flow back eventually to the river, like the original said. That only leaves three possible paths. But which one?

A tear spilled unbidden from her right eye. *Damn it, Tommy.*

He's done this before, you know, a voice in the corner of her mind whispered. *This isn't the first time.*

"Shut up," Alice whispered to herself. Tommy was the quiet one: reserved, sullen, thoughtful—sometimes a little brooding, but no trouble.

But that's not entirely true, is it?

"I said shut up," she said more sharply.

This isn't the first time, the voice insisted.

Notice how he only smiles when you're around?

Notice how unsettled you feel when he seems to stare into your soul, more like a lover than a brother?

You can't see because you don't want to see. Every goddamn time. You're an enabler.

Alice scoffed and shook her head. "Enabler? Yeah, okay."

Then why are you afraid to lower the bridge?

She shut out her mental echo, then hesitated. Now she really regretted drinking last night. Sighing, she closed her eyes and concentrated. It helped to visualise—extending oneself as a ghostly tendril snaking out along the tunnels, following the trail like a bloodhound on the scent. *This is stupid*, the cynical voice said, but Alice squeezed her eyes tighter, focusing solely on Tommy—memories of themselves as children, sitting cross-legged, staring into each other's eyes, souls playing hide and seek.

You can't hide from me, he'd say silently, a smile cracking on his face. *I can seeeee yooooouu.* Alice stifled a giggle.

No, you caaaaan't, she'd croon back. *You can't see my thoughts, not if I don't want you to.*

Tommy would smile—as a child he actually knew how—and touch his tawny eyes as he asked the inevitable question: *But why would you want to hide them from me?*

Her skin crawled, suddenly alive with subcutaneous worms. The tunnel splitting off diagonal left—that was where he went. She stood up and entered the drain.

Alice had to get down on her hands and knees again and crawl through the long, tight pipe, swatting aside more cobwebs and red backs. But the pull was getting stronger—she was moving in the right direction.

The pipe ended in yet another drop, albeit a short one. The concrete foundations had finally given way to ancient red brick. Milky-white calcium formations like drips of candle wax drips grew along the walls and miniature stalactites along the ceiling. A chain hung from a hasp bolted to the wall, though it was rusty and looked unsafe. But then there really wasn't much other choice.

Alice took the chain and gave it a few strong tugs. Satisfied it wouldn't snap, she rappelled down the short brick wall that became an uneven, crumbling slope. She let go of the chain and carefully picked her way down. Another drain waited at the bottom, this one big enough to stand upright in. She walked through to the other side and then consulted her map again.

No, no, this wasn't right either. This junction wasn't anywhere on the map. The path fanned off in three directions this time. The tunnels flowing off were some of the smallest yet. Worse, there was no graffiti in these tunnels—a bad sign. Alice's heartbeat began galloping in her chest. She was lost.

No, wait. There was graffiti, just two small pieces along a section of brick sticking out of the ceiling. Above the entrance to the leftmost pipe was a crude spray-painted skull—the blogs said skulls represented gas or a shortage of air, sometimes sewage. The second graffito, above the middle and rightmost pipes, was more ominous: *Abandon all hope.*

Christ, Alice thought, shivering again. *I have to call the police, the council. I can't do this. I can't do this alone.*

She turned, set on returning to the surface, then something lurched out of the shadows to her right, stopping her in her tracks.

"Ya lost, hunneh?" A man's voice burbled.

Alice yelped, leaping back. A matted beard and dirt-streaked face flew into her headlamp's beam. The man looked even more shocked than she felt. He shielded his eyes with a grimy hand, flashing a ring of crooked, brown teeth. Alice couldn't tell if he was smiling or sneering.

SAMSARA

The man took a step towards her, reaching out his other hand. The world around her seemed to move on its own and she found herself stumbling, rather than running, towards the deeper tunnels, instinct and fear carrying her away from the man blocking her path.

"What's wrong, hunneh?" he called after her, cackling in the croaky, breathless manner of a decades-long smoker. His laughter chased her down into the narrow pipe, resonating more malevolently the further she got away. She scuttled on hands and knees, her heartbeat so loud it seemed she could hear it in the pipes. Even with her slender frame she almost got stuck—and in her mind's eye she saw the vagrant's grimy hand catching at her ankles, dragging her back.

She pulled and squeezed, the brick scraping her back where her shirt had ridden up. Suddenly she shot free and tumbled out over the edge into a pitch-black chasm. She screamed, flying for what felt like a long time, somersaulting. Then she hit something hard—landing on her shoulder, bouncing, before her arse found solid ground again, sliding down a sheer angle. The darkness rushed up at her, whipped past like protoplasmic vines, yanking her deeper into an abyss without end.

The near-vertical drop abruptly ended, and Alice tumbled like a sack of old, soft potatoes onto flat, slimy brick. She hugged her knees and cried softly. Her left butt cheek felt tender and bruised. Her shoulder ached terribly but somehow it wasn't broken, but there was going to be a nasty bruise. She might not be able to even move it soon.

Oh Jesus, fuck. The floor seemed to drop out beneath her again. *Oh fucking hell, I've dropped so far down. I'm so far down, I don't even know where I am, I'm not gonna be able to get out here, oh fuck, I'm not—*

Alice burst into hoarse, hitching sobs. She cursed her twin, cursed the voice in her head. It wasn't the first time he'd drawn her into his messes before, she just didn't remember; she'd closed her eyes to him and made herself blind . . .

Then she realised it was far *too* dark. The light from her headlamp had gone out.

"No, no, no." Alice slipped the elastic headband off and slapped the lamp repeatedly. It didn't respond. She ran her fingers over the glass cover and felt sharp, jagged edges. "*Shit!*" she shouted and threw the headlamp into the darkness.

Alice reached into her front pocket for the spare torch. Hopefully it still worked. The thought that it might not stuck in her throat, unable to reach her brain for processing. She'd probably just curl into a ball and laugh until she died, madness and terror consuming her utterly.

She clicked the button. Nothing happened immediately, but a few seconds later, the globe warmed and sparked to life, a narrow beam piercing the gloom. Alice gave a short, shrill laugh. It didn't light much but it was better than nothing—a tiny ray of hope. An unsettlingly thick miasma of motes—dust, or maybe spores—passed through the beam. Alice pulled her shirt up over her nose and mouth and rose to her feet.

The tunnel was perhaps more accurately a massive subterranean vault, so wide that the beam couldn't find the walls, but the light flared across a solid ceiling some six metres above her. Alice sighed, shuddering. "Okay. Good."

SAMSARA

But nothing was good about this, really. She was stuck down in the deepest parts of Melbourne's sewer network, in uncharted tunnels, and nobody knew she was here. That part she regretted: she hadn't told anyone because Mum and her friends would have tried to dissuade her. Not because the tunnels were dangerous, but primarily because of Tommy. *He's bad news*, she could almost hear her friend Cecelia saying. Her mother would have used a whole array of euphemisms but the message remained just as clear. *Tommy's on his own path*, she'd told Alice once, looking at the carpet with heavy eyes. *Leave him be.* If only she'd listened . . . *Stupid, stupid, stupid.*

Now she might not be able to make it back up—the way down had been near vertical, the brickwork slimy or crumbling at its most accessible points. And that was before taking into account the worsening ache of her shoulder blade . . . Because of that fucking homeless guy, the only way left was down.

I can't believe I found someone living down here, Alice thought. *Wet, stinky, tons of spiders and rats . . . Are the tunnels really that better an option than sleeping on the streets?* Her heart sank, mired with guilt. Maybe he'd meant no harm, but survival instinct had seized her strings, turned her into a marionette animated by fear and adrenalin. The tunnels were scary enough without strangers jumping out of the shadows, even for a friendly howdy-do.

At least there was no chance of anyone living down this deep, except maybe giant rats. She shuddered at the thought that she might have to catch and kill one of the buggers for food if she couldn't get out.

She kept moving, paused at intervals as sudden movement and scratching, amplified by the cavernous spaces, gave her a start. The pitch blackness did nothing to dissuade her overactive imagination of horrors lurking beneath the city. She laughed, suddenly wishing she had never watched that horror film *The Tunnel*. Her flashlight found a trio of rats the size of cats, who scurried away in alarm, chittering.

Several hundred metres on, combing the flashlight along the roof, she spotted something. She pivoted her light to the far-left corner of the ceiling and slowly traced the beam across it. Symbols, but nothing like she'd ever seen before—a complicated, intricate cuneiform, red like seeping gashes. These tunnels were centuries old, but the markings seemed an anachronism from an even more distant time and place. They weren't leftover marks from the original builders, she felt certain of that. Her vision began to rumble and ache the longer she looked. There was something not quite right about them.

What are you afraid of? her echo said.

Tommy was down here. Her internal magnetics were going off like crazy, a compass arrow spinning in circles. She still sensed pain, but rather than the acute spark of screaming, anguished nerves it felt more like a dull, persistent ache through her skin and bones.

You know, don't you?

"Shut up."

Stop lying to yourself. All you need to do is reach out and see the truth.

But she wasn't ready for that. Opening the connection the little bit she had already had revealed more to her than she was comfortable acknowledging.

Another band of the slash-like markings appeared a little further down, then more, each band closer and closer together. A violent headache began pulsing right behind her eyes, beating like a kettledrum. And yet . . . she could read them. Not understand them, just read and articulate them.

It's not the same as being psychic, Tommy whispered in her memory, his mien too serious for a nine-year-old. *That's not what we are. We are one and the same, split down the middle—for us it's about feeling along the connection. You know, like those bridges that open and close over a river? That's what it is—lowering the bridge to let the thoughts and feelings flow freely like traffic over the river dividing us.*

I know what you know, and you know what I know.

Quashing the unease in her stomach, she spoke: "*Ya'ou teira m'kolra, teira dal'ku fioren.*" Her body convulsed with a violent shiver. *What the hell did I just say?*

Nothing happened. Except for the echo of dripping water and the titter of rats further back, nothing changed. *What were you expecting?* she chided herself. *Open sesame? Keep dreaming, girl.*

Alice continued down the tunnel. There were no more markings along the ceiling. The silence soon became stifling—even the constant drip of water had disappeared. A cool draught was making the skin on her arms prickle. *A draught!* That meant there was an exit somewhere along the line!

A freakish laugh suddenly cut through the pall, gurgling down the pipe. Alice jumped but made no sound, alarm killing the shriek in her throat. She shone the flashlight around, heart racing, trying to locate the source of the laugh. *Imagination playing tricks*, she tried to convince herself.

The light caught something smooth and pale slithering in the darkness. A slick, hairless head suddenly jerked up into the torch beam, a gap-toothed snarl twisted on a vaguely human face.

A piercing shriek pealed out behind her. Alice ran, the beam bouncing and zigzagging. More and more faces swam out of the gloom—wild-haired, bushy-faced, feral throngs hiding in the wings; naked bodies caked with grime and excrement, leering and giggling and snapping black and yellow teeth. The smell struck her like an invisible fist, a stomach-turning uppercut. How wrong she'd been, thinking no person would or could live this far down. Some lunged towards her, their swollen manhoods slapping against their thighs. All were men, insofar as the physical fact of their bodies, but their dilapidated appearance veered the implied fringes of humanity. The deeper she fled, the more vestigial and atavistic their resemblance to men became.

She ran, driving through cramping muscles, for fear of what would happen if she stopped.

And suddenly she was falling again, scrabbling vainly against the deep's billowing folds, crazed laughter chasing her over the precipice like a waterfall. In that moment she hoped the fall would kill her, Tommy be damned.

Something always flings you apart.

Alice stopped screaming after the third pause for breath, silently praying for the sudden crack, the brief agony of crushed bones and pulverised meat.

After a fall too long and deep to be part of Melbourne anymore, something spongey and moist cushioned her impact. It made an unnatural gasping, flatulent sound as she landed and bounced onto

48

harder ground. Alice stared up into the unyielding gloom for a long time. Fuck Tommy, fuck their connection. You just couldn't save some people. If she was going to die down here, alone in the dark, the least she could do was die with a curse on her lips.

Every time.

It hadn't always been this way. They'd been so close. But then that closeness had reached creepy, invasive depths. Tommy crossed a line there was no coming back from.

Alice had been dating Ryan for over a year. He hadn't pressured her once for sex, and after a year she'd finally been ready. She'd waited a lot longer than Cecelia or any of her other friends. It seemed rare for a woman these days to still be a virgin at twenty years old. She wasn't afraid; she just didn't want to waste it. She wanted her first time to be magic, with someone worthy of her; but part of her was like a starved animal, electric, ready to jump his bones. She hoped he was as good a lover as he was good-looking and kind.

All that changed shortly after Ryan slid inside her, when she felt Tommy's eyes glaring from within, a parasite looking out through her lens; felt his rage burning as Ryan moaned and thrusted. She'd recoiled and pushed him off, his touch as unwelcome as winter frost. Tommy had never done anything like that before, or since, but it frightened her, him watching jealously like a spurned lover. She'd not been able to look into Ryan's eyes again without seeing Tommy. She broke up with Ryan without explanation, stopped answering his texts and eventually blocked his number, and never saw or spoke to him again.

Even now the memory of it stung, but back then she'd had bigger problems to deal with than scorn and heartbreak.

From that day on, the bridge had been permanently raised; the link between twins severed. She'd moved out of the family home within a week, moved into Cecelia's house on the other side of the city. But even that wasn't enough—she took to the bottle to try and wipe the memory of Tommy's invasion from her mind and almost lost her job as a staff writer for *The Age*. Russell had spared her on the proviso she quit drinking, and she had, until last night. She almost hadn't come at all.

Last night she felt his pain and terror break through her defences, leap across the raised bridge. She hadn't spoken to him for almost two years, hadn't even allowed herself to think of him, until Mum had called her a week ago. The regret of permitting him even in her thoughts again was almost instantaneous.

"Fuck you, Tommy," Alice said softly, too numb and exhausted for tears.

She sat up and groped around for the flashlight but came up empty. Then the tears finally did come, scorching and savage, her body hitching in despair.

Eventually she wiped her streaming face and sat up. *Stop it, girl. What use are tears? No-one's coming to save you, so stop sobbing like someone will. You gotta save yourself.*

Then Alice noticed a faint corona of light radiating down the far end of the passageway, highlighting its irregular outline. She let out a frayed laugh. *No way! Light!* Suddenly, she was crawling, faster and faster, ignoring the sting of bruised muscles and scraped knees. The light grew brighter—definitely an exit of some sort. She didn't even care where it led. The first light she'd seen in what felt like eternity.

SAMSARA

The bricks disappeared, giving way to gritty, pebble-strewn rock. Perhaps the man-made tunnels flowed out into a natural system of tunnels deep in the rock, allowing stormwater to flow into an underground basin. It seemed unlikely that workers would have burrowed and built this deep. Would it be a way out, though, or a dead end? It almost didn't matter. She thought back to how deep she'd fallen, how darkly her hope had been eclipsed—but simply knowing she would see light again, liberated of the claustrophobia of the reeking tunnels, she could die happy. She held onto that grain of hope, however small or irrational. Hope—that last bastion for desperados everywhere suddenly struck illiterate, unable to read the writing on the wall.

At last the tunnel ended, opening into a massive cavern. Jagged islands rose from the floor and sharp, peculiar formations twisted overhead like chandeliers of knives. The brightness of the light ebbed away, revealing shadowy creek beds and alleyways set against pockets of reddish light, their source obscured by rocky shelves and columns. Alice sighed in relief. But as she stood listening to the rhythmic squelching sounds and eerie whistle roaring in the cavern's throat, her elation began to fade. Her stomach shivered, uneasy.

Alice picked her way among the alleyways, allowing the draught to guide her. But every time she caught a whiff of that pestilent wind— like a combination of rotting meat, shit and sickness—part of her screamed to run the other way. But going back wasn't an option. Besides, if stormwater and God knew what else flowed down here, of course it was going to stink. *Stop being stupid.*

Then something else beyond the breeze moaned amongst the rock formations—a moan that sounded decidedly more human, weak and constant with pain. *Tommy!*

Alice ran towards the source, squeezing through a narrow gap in the rock. On the other side were two braziers piled with glowing coals, which was strange enough, but nowhere as horrifying as what she saw next. Her hands flew up to her mouth, her eyes bulging. *Get out of here, got to get out of here*, her internal voice screamed. It was she, not Tommy, who was in danger, and it was no longer by insistence of her environment—struggling against darkness and dangerous precipices. No, someone*, something* within these tunnels, meant to do her harm, perhaps the same as they had for Tommy . . . She could still feel him, hurting but *alive.* For how long, though . . .

Beyond the braziers, dozens of iron spears had been driven into the ground at odd angles, forming a snaking line. Misshapen forms writhed in agony, impaled upon the shafts, moaning and gurgling as if their insides were slush. Somehow, despite extreme deformity and terrible, certainly lethal wounds, they were all somehow still alive—though alive may have been a stretch. Their eyes rolled up to the ceiling, effectively brain-dead, scratching for Heaven with no respite.

More disturbing still, each form was fused to another in freakish, disgusting ways. A grotesque gallery of amalgamated flesh and bone, with deformities so universally monstrous, so aberrant, so debilitating . . . It was impossible that these were natural disfigurations. No . . . *These were made.* An icy finger traced down her spine at the certainty of it . . . An infant fused at the hip and head, a bulbous Neanderthal brow creating an overly large gap between a pair of eyes, mewling from a single lopsided mouth. A brother and sister merged like entwined lovers, faces joined together by smooth pink scar tissue, hip and leg bones fused like a single skeletal finger covered in a thin membrane of skin. A hideous mass of pink gelatinous flesh with discombobulated features spread throughout like shotgun pellets—an eye here, a hand and a warped breast there; a nose among clumps of stiff black hair. A horrifying spectrum of inconceivable deformity and suffering spread out like victims of Vlad the Impaler. But the connection was clear: *twins.* Maybe Tommy hadn't come here of his own will after all . . . Maybe he'd been lured—just like she'd been lured, her twin brother the bait . . .

Alice stumbled away, then keeled over, vomit exploding from her trembling guts. It was one thing to accept the risk of dying down here—the bastion of hope had never been real anyway—but now even the delusion of escape had been torn to the ground, every brick dismantled. This, she couldn't process this. She hadn't thought there could be much worse than being crippled and dying alone in the tunnels, food for the rats, but now she knew better. It could *always* be worse—wriggling on one of those spikes in terrible pain, babbling like a lobotomised idiot.

I have to keep moving. In this horrible place, even suicide lost its desperate appeal. If they could keep these things alive beyond the point of certain death, perhaps they could bring her back too . . .

And that's when she knew: she wasn't under Melbourne anymore. This wasn't even Earth anymore. It was no use denying her instinct. Somehow she had fallen so far, crossed some crucial threshold and landed into Hell—or else she'd gone completely mad.

Stop it. Don't lose your head, Alice, we'll get out of this—

53

Too late, the echo in her head whispered. *Over and over, and yet you never learn . . . Samsara, baby. When will you finally wake up?*

Heavy footsteps marched towards her position. Alice pushed herself up against a wall and peeked out. She couldn't see the newcomers but knew there had to be at least two of them. And that she'd be in deep shit if they found her.

She doubled back past the impaled abominations and hid behind a rocky butte. Tommy's voice abruptly spoke in her mind: *They know you're there.* His voice was calm. *No use running.*

Where are you? she asked, panic setting in. The footfalls were getting closer, so close now she could hear their owners' snuffled breathing. *Tommy? Tommy?!*

He didn't answer.

The footsteps stopped about two metres away from her hiding place. The snuffling continued, like a bulldog gasping for air. *Are they trying to sniff me out?* The thought almost made her heart stop. She peered around the rock as the creatures scanned the creek bed in the other direction—thick, muscular torsos with four arms, each tipped in claws like shards of onyx. Their facial features were blunt, with a stubby, compacted nose and four beady black eyes almost swallowed by thick-spurred eye sockets. Great yellow tusks jutted out of the upper and lower jaws, separated by rows of smaller, pointed teeth. They looked like a combination of orcs and some stupid character from one of Tommy's old *Mortal Kombat* games.

Alice waited breathlessly as several moments passed. The creatures soon moved back from whence they came and Alice let out a soft, shaky breath. A single tear spilled from her right eye. *Too close—way too close.*

There was a brief, loud crash, then the cavern fell silent again, except for the soft groaning of the impaled twins. Still Alice could not break her paralysis.

A plume of dust and fine shale rained down. Alice screamed as the shadows unfolded, pregnant with unnatural life, thick limbs unhinging, the feeble light of the coals glimmering on black eyes and salivating lips. A long, bubbling growl, then a chunky, three-fingered hand clamped around her face, shutting out the nightmare and suffocating her screams—then yanked her up into the darkness.

It's better not to fight, Tommy whispered.

"Where do you want this thing?"

"Near her feet for now."

"Is this the specimen you wanted, Your Worship?"

"She is the *specimen, Xograr. The final subject."*

"She doesn't look so special?" another voice said.

The dominant voice gave a long, crocodilian growl. Even with her eyes shut, Alice could sense the other creatures' anxiety.

"Forgive Hingas, Master," said Xograr, the one with the baritone voice. *"He did not mean offence. He simply meant she looks just like the others."*

"Yes!" cried Hingas. *"Yes, yes, exactly!"*

The master cursed—in English!—and Alice realised the conversation had not been spoken in English, but in some alien, unspeakable tongue she understood all the same. The same tongue as the runes from the tunnel. But that didn't make a lick of sense . . .

I know what you know, and you know what I know.

One of the monsters shuffled uncomfortably. Alice suddenly felt eyes upon her. *"She stirs, Lord Morgaul,"* said Xograr.

"Good," the master said. *"Xograr, Crakzir, you may leave. Hingas—"*

"Yes, Master?" Hingas answered, high and uneven.

"You remain. I have another task for you."

Hingas said no more but Alice sensed his trepidation. The creature shuffled to the wings, awaiting the master's bidding.

"Open your eyes. I know you can understand me."

Alice squeezed her eyes tighter, squirming on the stone slab. She willed herself invisible from that terrible, soul-shaking voice making a mockery of human speech. Several moments passed in tense silence, save for the monster's long, crackling exhalations.

"Open your eyes, Alice. I will not hurt you."

Her left eye peeled open, daring not to defy the creature a second time, and almost immediately snapped it shut for the horror that greeted her. Even so, the charnel house seared itself into the darkness beneath her eyelids like a gory bas relief: scarred, fused abominations threaded along a single serpentine length of chain that hung along the chamber eaves, drooling and jerking spasmodically. The two burly monsters—Xograr and Crakzir—were identical to the ones who had captured her; Hingas was smaller and lankier, and only had two spindly arms. Then there was the Master himself—

"LOOK AT ME."

She shook her head but her eyes creaked open against her will. This time her eyelids bolted open and stayed open, as if held open by invisible forceps. The demon's visage burnt itself into her mind, so

56

bright and terrifying she thought she might never sleep again. Her inevitable death was a mercy. That God could permit such a thing to exist—for surely this hell, these creatures, must be proof He too existed—made her wonder why Christians were always banging on about a generous, loving God. There was nothing loving or giving about this being, except perhaps in its capacity to inflict cruelty.

Stooped over it still stood at over three metres tall, with a thick chest and bulging veined arms, ending in giant long-fingered hands with talons as long and sharp as *wakizashi*. Skin mottled black-grey, scarified with the same slashing marks as the writing in the tunnels. Bony protrusions tore out of its brow like a crown of interlocking spikes. Smouldering coals for eyes glowed in meaty charcoal pits gouged out of its gargantuan head. Slender, razor-sharp teeth the length of an adult's forearm in its grinning mouth. *No wings, though,* she observed. *Not even stumps. This one didn't even make it to Heaven. Got "Made in Hell" written all over it.* She almost laughed in lunatic terror.

"Am I so horrible to look upon?" Morgaul asked, croaking reptilian laughter. *"Yes, I suppose I am. But you know my heart, Alice, my soul. You've always known. Haven't you?"*

Tommy, a child again, staring into her eyes with uncanny intensity. The adult Alice gasped.

I know what you know, and you know what I know.

"Tommy?"

A slow gurgle rose from the demon's throat, a monstrous chortle. Alice dared hope for a moment she had misread. That hope was dashed the moment Morgaul smiled.

Alice's mouth fell open. "How is this even *possible*? I—I felt you! You were in pain!"

"Yes. I am still in pain—but I understand your meaning. Even after centuries this form still anguishes, searing. But not nearly as badly as my spirit."

"Centuries? Tommy—"

"Time in this plane does not conform to humanity's perception of it." The demon growled, his coal-eyes flaring brighter. *"And do not use my mortal name again. I am Morgaul now—though I am still your brother."*

"How—I—I don't understand any of this. This place, what you are, why . . ."

"I went searching for answers to questions and mysteries that have vexed me relentlessly; this feeling that my whole life I circled around and around, removed from my own soul, frustrated and incomplete. I could not have known, Alice, just how right I was. One piece of the eternal puzzle continuously eluded me. That part is always lost in the cycle, when life yields to death, and then death to life again."

"What are you talking about?" she demanded. But so many times the same uncanny thoughts had crept into her mind as she drowned her sorrow and memories in a bottle of vodka, trying to expel the insidious truth . . .

"We have been doing this forever, sweet sister. Over centuries and millennia we have done the same dance, over and over, lifetime after lifetime—born and reborn, divided and divided again, orbiting but then flung apart by circumstance. We never remember, until the pain becomes so great that I can no longer bear it . . . Then the pain opens a vault storing countless lifetimes' worth of memories. Every

lifetime I have gone searching—how to bring our divided soul back together—and every time it has ended in failure. You have run from me. You have feared where I have longed and ached, and no knowledge could deliver the answers to our eternal dilemma. Then . . ."

"Then . . ?"

"In the weeks before I disappeared, I discovered secret, forbidden knowledge that answered the question of sundered souls, and how to repair them. But the means to see it through were terrifying—you cannot begin to comprehend the risk, the likelihood of failure. I almost did fail. But after you shut me out this time, I could no longer bear it. It was worth a thousand hells and every agony under the stars just to try. I heard rumours of secret ways into other realms. Luckily for me I was not the first traveller to the underworld, though their objectives were far less noble than mine."

"The runes—they opened up the doorway when I spoke them, didn't they?"

Morgaul nodded. "Think of them not as doorways but permits of transition. License to swap one's mundane reality for another—a different language of creation. All who speak that language can touch, see, smell, even kill any other from it—like ghosts made into flesh. Our old world is like that now—as incorporeal as a phantom, and likewise us to it. We belong to this physical reality now."

"Hell."

Morgaul smiled condescendingly. "If you like. This is a place of immense cruelty, indeed, but it is not the Hell Men dream and fear. It is something else entirely, and far worse than any dream of Men. But if thinking of it this way makes understanding simpler . . ."

"So you came here and became a demon."

"I did not come with that intention. I was a human fool blinded by single-mindedness and heartache. I admit I did not think about how I might actually make such a thing come to pass. I came here, blind, lovesick—and then they took me. Ripped my soul like a wick from a candle—an abstraction made into a physical, malleable thing. They tortured me, raped me endlessly; devoured me and shat me back out and then remade me to begin all over again . . . Never have I known such pain. Even now, the memory of it burns. But after centuries of torment and breaking, my mortal life but an insignificant dream, I remembered you. And that memory of you unearthed the bones of my purpose from the misty grave of forgetfulness. Rage so bright as to scorch the fiends to their pith. My wrath, doffed of its human impotence, caught this realm like a spark to tinder." As Morgaul spoke, Alice noticed Hingas shifting uncomfortably in her periphery, as if he'd heard the story before—as if perhaps he had only marginally *survived* it . . .

"I murdered, I burned—I raped the demons and paid them back a hundred times their cruelty. I gorged on black blood and tangy flesh. So consumed by vengeance and memory, I did not see how it sent me back to my true path, how my feasting changed *me."*

Alice felt her gullet shorten, tasting acid at the back of her mouth. The ball of ice in her belly sent cold waves through her limbs, as she watched something like nostalgia wash over her brother's face.

"I became Lord of this place, overthrowing the one who called himself Prince before. Although intoxicated on bloodlust as I was, I wanted to no part in the mission of this realm. I split this branch off from the tree—what you see now is a pocket reality, a bubble of space-

time floating independently on the greater chain of order and chaos. I ripped apart Hell to bring us back together, make a place for us. It's the only thing I ever cared about."

"Yes." A tear slid down Alice's cheek. She'd always known the lengths he'd go, the depths of depravity he'd plumb to reunite them, though she never imagined *this*. A sense of things constantly in motion, repeated but unremembered, never able to place or shake the feeling. *Lifetimes . . .* Every lifetime Tommy had been working towards this end, endlessly searching and abasing himself, always a little closer.

Alice slumped back against the rough slab, eyes passing over the gnashing abominations adorning the walls. "So what now?" she asked, resigned.

Morgaul turned and circled to a massive, gleaming cauldron at the end of the slab, hefting it effortlessly as if it were no more than a paperweight. *"In the centuries I passed here, I learned the answer to the riddle: why are some of us separated, two vessels carrying portions of one soul? It is because the soul is too strong, too powerful, we rival the architects of creation—so out of fear we are* unmade, broken. This cauldron is one such forge, in whose caldera souls are made and unmade, fused and unfused."* He flashed a savage smile. *"Don't you see? The enigma only proves it is our destiny to restore the fragmented soul—to rule and exercise the birthright of power denied to us!"*

Alice shook her head, squeezing her fists tighter. What hope was there in fighting anymore? Her voice was a tired whisper: "Then do it. Unite us. Bring our souls together if it will bring you peace."

Morgaul stood fully upright, gaining an extra metre in height, and let out a crackling, rapturous breath. *"Hingas,"* he called, gesturing toward the cauldron.

Hingas lowered his bulbous head, his skinny form shrinking as he moved, then stopped in front of the cauldron. He was trembling. *"Master—"*

Morgaul brought his massive claws around Hingas's neck and ripped it open, pulling the demon's head free. Black blood gushed out of his neck stump. The body pitched over and fell upon the rim, almost falling in until Morgaul buried his claws deep into Hingas's torso, holding him back. The cauldron filled rapidly, an oily sea rising within its great brass belly. Then Morgaul flung the exsanguinated corpse against the wall, striking one of the chained abominations. The hanging creature pitched forward, dangling out from the wall by the chain threaded through its side, but did not fall.

Then Morgaul fixed Alice with his hot coal eyes. *"Reuniting the two halves is not enough. We must be one b—"*

But she knew—she already knew. "Don't say it. Don't you dare fucking say it."

"We must be one flesh also, sister. Vicissitude—flesh-crafting—is a difficult art to master. Do not judge me by my failures. I have practised now for centuries and my skill has improved—"

Alice snorted derisively but could not hide the horror rippling through her body, like swarms of flesh-burrowing beetles gnawing towards her bones. "I don't see how it could get much worse."

"Flesh is weak and corruptible—our shell will never be as pure as our spirit. But where the vessel is imperfect the soul will be strong!"

"No, Tommy! I don't want this. You have no right!"

SAMSARA

"You think to lecture me on rights*?!"* Morgaul snarled. *"Is it not my right to be whole? Tell me truthfully that you do not feel as broken as I?"*

"We were close," Alice replied, "until you became possessive and pervy and watched me fuck my boyfriend! We do have a special connection, but that's never enough for you. You are endless hunger—endlessly insatiable. It will never be enough, no matter how much I give." She closed her eyes, digging into impossible memories rising like mirages from the sand. "Every time *you* have torn us apart. *You.* Not the gods, not fate, not a defect in our mother's womb, *you.* You try to own me, possess the whole for yourself. You think we're two parts of one whole. But you're proof of just how wrong you are. We couldn't be any more different, you and I. You don't own this— you don't own *me.*" She jabbed her finger on her chest, glaring defiantly at her brother. "My soul is my own—and even if it is broken, it doesn't fucking matter. It's *my* portion." Alice sneered, almost forgetting her fear. "You're the one who needs me. I'm whole enough. I've been doing just fine without you."

Morgaul's mouth twisted, showing a barrier of interlocked, scissoring teeth. *"You lie. You can't hide your thoughts and feelings from me. Don't you see? Your lies and denial—the same objections and reversals, the same longing, in every cycle and yet we never learn. You never learn. You are the cause of our torment. This is our samsara, Alice: our endless wandering. Finally, I have the power to break the cycle—Castor and Pollux, the divided Gemini remade, body and soul—and still, still you resist! WHY?"*

"Because you're incapable of happiness," Alice answered, shaking her head. "You'll always be empty. You'd do all this, change us, and then what? What then, huh?"

And for the briefest of moments, she sensed doubt flicker across her brother's mind.

"No," he growled, tendrils of smoke rising from his burning eyes. *"I will be whole. We both will."* Morgaul lifted the sloshing cauldron and moved around to her side, gesturing the bowl towards her. *"Drink."*

Alice turned her head away. The demon's blood smelled like a soup of dead seagulls and dissolving sharks; a frothing black sea too salty and putrescent to sustain life. Her stomach flipped, ready to eject from her body. "Fuck off," she said.

Morgaul exhaled impatiently, his breath a fetid carrion wind. *"I won't kill you,"* he snarled, *"but I am not opposed to . . . persuading you into compliance by whatever means necessary. I will pay any price to see our reunification complete."*

"I won't drink it."

"Very well." Morgaul set the cauldron down and lumbered to the other side of the chamber. *"Gavage it is, then."*

A clang of chains followed by a crash sent echoes pealing across the cavern. They both looked to the far-left corner of the room, just behind her slab. The hanging abomination—the one knocked askew by Hingas's carcass—had finally fallen from its perch. The chain had pulled taut like a tightrope, threatening to bring the rest of the display down like a string of poorly hung Christmas lights.

Morgaul grunted and returned to his business. He came back with a short, wide length of copper pipe. *"This will hurt, but you have left me little choice. But it will be over soon, I promise. Then we will be together, one flesh to be shaped as putty however we wish."*

"No!" Alice screamed, leaping off the slab. Morgaul's claw ripped through the stone as easily as a pile of autumn leaves a moment later.

"It will do you no good to run, sister," Morgaul said, his voice smiling in lieu of his hardened countenance. *"I made this place. Wherever you run, however far you get ahead, I know every corner and crevice. I will catch you. And I will not be kind."*

Morgaul trudged closer, his huge shadow swallowing her. She shied away, instinctively closing her eyes. He was right. She'd never escape. The best she could hope for was he'd overestimate himself and accidentally kill her in the process. Even then, that was no guarantee his mission would be over . . .

The chains rattled. Morgaul was too focused on grabbing her to heed it.

Her brother suddenly made a gagging, choking sound. Alice's eyes snapped open. Hingas still laid dead but the body from the wall was no longer inert. The abomination was on its feet and garrotting her brother with a loop of chain. It held the makeshift garrotte with its huge right hand—made from two hands and fingers asymmetrically fused together—while its left grasped the other end of the chain and pulled. The abomination grunted as the chain dragged through its torso, shredding its protruding guts. The string of other deformed creatures fell to the floor, pulled loose of their display, spilling dust and broken rock in their wake.

The abomination fixed her with a single embryonic eye—a watery yellow zygote not quite divided. Its mind pried into hers, a mental voice livid with desperation. *Go! We will hold him!* Even as he spoke, the other flesh-crafted nightmares moved in, hungry for revenge even if their warped faces could hardly express it. *Follow the winding path up onto the escarpment,* the abomination instructed. *There is an altar and some statues beyond a courtyard. The nearest gateway lies not far from there. Say the words and it will open.*

"But I don't know the—"

Go, now! We don't have much time! He cannot be allowed to do this to anyone else!

Alice stared agape for a few more heartbeats, trying to process how quickly the tables had turned. One of the aberrations shoved her forward and her legs moved of their own accord.

"NOOOOO!" Morgual screamed, rumbling the cavern. Then, in her mind: *Don't do this! I love you!*

You don't know a thing about it, Alice sent back, never missing a beat.

Morgaul screeched in torment. She heard something like the chain breaking—or exploding—followed by a sound like overripe fruit bursting against a wall. She did not think she could push her body any harder but was happy when her limbs obeyed, her legs like two titanium pistons, seemingly inexhaustible. Confused demonic faces whipped past her; a claw or two absently reached out to catch her and missed. She dodged and focused on the long, serpentine path rising ahead of her. The escarpment jutted out several floors above, a rocky mandible opening into another cavern beyond the ceiling.

She'd gotten a good head start now, but the element of surprise was gone. The demons knew she was loose and Morgaul was in pursuit. She could hear his thunderous footfalls closing the gap, feel them vibrating through the ground. His screams roared throughout the cavern.

The path became steeper and more difficult, but Alice did not stop. She rounded the hairpin turn, driving through fatiguing muscles. She glanced down. Her brother barrelled after her, swatting and cutting down anything too stupid or shocked to get out of the way. *Stop running, Alice! Please!*

Alice reached the next bend. An ugly, burly demon blocked her path. She faltered, skidding and nearly tripping, then charged, ramming the huge creature aside like it was nothing. She whooped and screamed, *"I'm the Juggernaut, bitch!"* But her moment of lunacy died as Morgaul's coal-eyes appeared over the edge of the escarpment behind her, flaring incandescent. The air shimmered and distorted as he roared. She must be close now—she sensed his panic beneath the trappings.

"STOP RUNNING! THERE IS NO ESCAPE!"

But he knew that *she* knew he was lying. There was a way out, and he feared she might just make it. Galvanised, Alice urged her burning thighs forward, leaping over outcrops, darting past pillars.

A vast courtyard opened before her, littered with charred skeletons, random bones, and oozing, indistinguishable piles of rotting mush. A massive stone dais rose on the other side, flanked by dead brass braziers and a smooth rock wall at the rear. A pair of colossal statues of her brother's monstrous form presided over all. *This must be where they come to worship him—stroke his ego while he gluts himself.* The thought made her sick. For all his problems, for all his obsessiveness, Morgaul was not the brother she knew—he was

67

too far gone to bring Tommy back. Even if he or she wanted to, there was no way to undo what had been done.

Then she remembered her echo: *Something always flings you apart.* Images exploded like fireworks, a kaleidoscopic clockwork of wheeling memories and forgotten cycles, and she saw him and his atrocities. Stabbing her husband to death in jealous rage beneath the colonnade of Hephaestus's temple, pushing her away as she screamed and tried to stop him. Learning he had bribed the priest Pachal Ix, screaming as the priests decapitated her husband atop Kulkulkan's temple and flung his head bouncing down the temple steps. Her fiancé, Gideon Pearce, ending their betrothal after receiving her brother's letter 'warning' him she planned to divorce him and fleece him of his family fortune. Countless lives across human history exploded through her mind's eye, Tommy's obsession with reunification driving them apart every time.

He'd always been a monster—she'd just turned a blind eye to it. She always *forgot.* The only difference now was he wore the right skin to match the soul beneath it.

Alice's eyes darted, her heart in full gallop. She expected to find the gateway behind the dais, but it wasn't there. Of course it wasn't— nothing was ever so easy. It was nowhere to be seen and Morgaul was closing in by the second. She closed her eyes, silencing her echo's protests, and reached out into Morgaul's mind. *I know what you know, and you know what I know. Now, where is the fucking gate?*

Her brother, taken aback by the sudden invasion, stopped in his tracks. He resisted, tried to push back, but she already had her fingers in under the skin, pulling it back like pork crackling. *And . . .* there it was—hidden within an inconspicuous hollow just off to the left! She started toward it, letting out a disbelieving laugh as her eyes fell upon the ring of red cuneiform.

The cavern shook as if with thunder, blasting away all thought and bravado. Morgaul strode into view, upper lip twitching. *"I told you how this would end."*

"How do you do it? After all you've said and done, after ruining every life I've ever had, how do you live with yourself? You think pairing with me will miraculously make you better, more whole?" She stared at the runes carved into his flesh and laughed, hard and cynical. "*Nothing* can do that. Only this time I know for sure. There's no saving you, Tommy. This is the last time we do the dance."

"Yes. It is."

Alice reached out and an invisible hand caught her probing mind by the throat. *"Don't,"* Morgaul grated. *"You can't see my thoughts if I don't want you to."*

Alice grinned wolfishly. "But why would you want to hide them from me, Tommy?"

Morgaul's eyes bolted open as Alice grit her teeth and forced with all her mental strength. His defences crumpled, disarmed by his surprise. She found the words for the exit gate that he had been guarding—so close to the surface, too, the fool—and pulled herself back. She looked back and tried to speak, but Morgaul roared, *"NO!"* and charged.

Alice rifled through her memories like a flipbook, rewinding to when they were young. Tommy always dwelt on that, cherishing their childhood as some sacred, infallible moment of unity. In his perverse mind it was the truest of times, unsullied by boundaries and ideas of individual self. And yet it wasn't always so rosy—he liked to forget that.

They'd still fought, especially as they grew older: one time he tried to bully her into playing the mind game, when they were ten; only she didn't want to play that anymore because she didn't want him knowing her secrets. He'd gotten mad—he already knew the secret, he said: she had a crush on Will McNamara in her class. Tommy had called Will a dick and said only sluts thought about boys—and that's when she'd turned her little hands into claws and raked them across his face. Oh, how he'd bawled!

Claws would do no good against this creature, but *memory,* the *proof* of its falseness could still cut so deep . . .

Alice lashed out, flinging the memory like a morning star, smashing inside his demon skull. The demon screeched and reeled back, burying his face in his giant hands. Wasting no time, Alice spun and read the symbols: *"Ya'ou dairash yutac miru, teira eendu mu'ku rei—Ahhhh!"*

Bolts of pain sheared through her shoulder and back like a trio of hot knives. Morgaul's scimitar claws raked across bone, cleaving muscle and peeling flesh like an onion skin, but Alice was already running, screaming in rage and defiance against the pain, throttling the instinct to collapse. Morgaul made a second swipe but came just short, inches from snipping her foot off at the ankle. *"NOOOOOO!"*

He was almost on top of her, but she was within strides of the gateway. Had the damn thing opened? There was no way to tell.

Morgaul went for a third swipe. He was right on top of her now. It'd be lucky if he didn't kill her—or maybe a shame. She passed into the rune-rimmed cervix of the portal, sensing no discernible shift—

A deafening *BANG* followed by a shockwave sent Alice crashing to her feet. She stared over her glistening exposed shoulder and her jaw dropped. Despite the coal-eyes and monstrous mouth, the face that stared back at her did not belong to Morgaul. Utter astonishment had wiped his face clean of its belligerence—it was just the face of a stunned, wounded little boy. Alice let out an uncertain, disbelieving laugh.

Her brother screamed on the other side, hammering relentlessly on an invisible membrane separating their worlds. *Languages of creation*, he'd called them, exchanging one tangible reality for another at the expense of the former. Only he had pinned himself to his own dimension—the language inscribed into his flesh prevented him from crossing over. He had depended on her ignorance all along to bring her to heel, but he'd underestimated her. Cycles of mistakes and wilful blindness had led to this conclusion. Now she was free.

Alice slumped against the rock wall and cried, relief washing over her. She tuned out her brother's muffled shrieking. She didn't have long—she was bleeding hard and even if there was a way back to the surface from here, she wouldn't survive the climb. The darkness was already swirling down to take her. But she surrendered to it on her own terms, which was more than she could say for Tommy. He'd condemned himself to a hell of his own making, the worst kind imaginable. He had made himself immortal, so he had broken the cycle after all; just not in the way he had hoped. Maybe this really was the end of it. The final time they did the dance . . .

Fuck you, Tommy, Alice thought, wondering if he could still hear her. Her sense of him was already beginning to fade. Perhaps they weren't two halves at all: just one whole scraping and overcompensating for an empty vessel. And she had not given an inch this time. The crimes against her past selves were avenged.

I die here in the dark, but not with a curse on my lips. I rejoice. Your stranglehold on me is finished. I die as my own person.

She closed her eyes and smiled. It didn't matter if there wasn't another round after this. The prospect of another life was exhausting—but as her life ebbed away into the rocks and dirt, she dared dream of a life, just one life, of hope, love and joy; a world of possibilities, open now that her endless wandering had finally come to an end. For in that sleep of death what dreams may come, she could not say, until it all came circling around again . . .

About the Author:

Marcus Turner is a speculative, horror, and dark fantasy author from Melbourne, Australia, where he lives with his wife Tita and his two children. He was first published in Deadset Press' Beginnings anthology with his story, 'A Spark of Youth', in November 2018, and has since been featured in several other anthologies. He is a keen gamer, metalhead, avid reader of Batman and Judge Dredd comics, and is a little more obsessed with Cthulhu and all things Cthulhu Mythos than is probably healthy. Marcus cites Clive Barker, Stephen King, H.P. Lovecraft, Edgar Allen Poe, George R.R. Martin and R. Scott Bakker as the major influences on his own writing. He currently working on his first novel, entitled Land of the Righteous. *You can connect with him via the following media:*

Facebook: www.facebook.com/MarcusTurnerWriter/
Twitter: @FuryThePhoenix
Website: marcusturnerauthor.com

Gemini Memory

M. R. Mortimer

The door screeched open and I climbed gingerly into the beat-up old Gemini coupe. The girl behind the wheel looked at me with the hunger of a wolf and the disdain of a politician. Before I was seated—before I had my belt on—she put her foot to the floor. The gravel sprayed, the tyres squealed, and the old Holden leaped into action. Several bright spots shone low in the sky ahead of us. I recognised the constellation, but it was too bright, and in the wrong place.

I had been running from all sorts of things when I rolled the ute on the back road from Urinquinty. Why did I get in the Gemini and abandon the ute? Well, it wasn't mine. I think she already knew that when she spun around and picked me up after witnessing the wreck in her rear-view mirror. I looked at the girl, trying to ignore the too bright stars that still shone ahead of us.

"Uhm, thanks for picking me up," I stammered, unsure of what else to say.

She glanced sidelong at me, a smirk creeping across her face like a lizard on a rock. She laughed. It was a barked out laugh, how I imagined a hyena might sound.

"My name is Simon," I said.

Another glance. Another smirk. No laughter this time. Thank Christ.

"So what's your name?"

Silence.

Well, this conversation was going nowhere. I rested my chin on my hand and stared at the parched landscape as it thundered by, the scrub a green-grey blur against red soil.

Thinking about it, this was no ordinary girl. Her clothes were odd, too. Though they were dusty, the colours weren't faded and the fabric had little in the way of wear. But the style was thirty years old.

And the car was as much an enigma. The outside had the evidence of age and an accident, one that had seen the car roll, several times from the look of it. The paint work was worn and scraped, and rust blistered through in a number of places. The wing mirrors were gone, the roof bent, the bonnet buckled, but somehow it still drove. If I was thinking clearly I would have felt safer outside that thing than in it. But the inside was immaculate, as if it had just rolled off the lot. It was, almost mystical in its beauty. I felt like I was the first person to sit in the passenger seat, and I was probably going to be the last.

Without warning, the driver spoke. Her voice whisked past my ears like the wind outside the Gemini.

"So, why'd yer steal that ute?"

Caught, I looked at her.

"I bin travelin' this road fer years. I seen that car drivin' around a bit in that time and it weren't never you drivin' the thing."

She had the line on me all right.

"Don't yer worry 'bout me. I like'm bad."

I looked at her and she turned back to the road. The smirk was gone. She seemed in that moment, a sad image. My heart felt briefly sorry for her and I wasn't sure why. Then her composure was back. The lizard had returned, to guard her emotions from the strange boy who rolled other people's utes. Those stars in front of us seemed to be glaring at me, judging me.

"So? Why?"

Her voice made it clear I'd better answer her.

"I have to get to Albury. A mate's been stitched up and he needs my help."

"There's always a mate," she said. "That's how it was fer us, that time."

The sadness was there again so I turned back to the passing scrub. None of it was familiar, those rocks past the bend, the old farm gate, we'd passed none of the familiar landmarks. I hadn't seen any intersections, no strange turns. It felt like the road was being stretched.

"Well, we ain't gunna get ter Albury tonight," she said.

Her words surprised me. It wasn't a long drive to Albury. Even so, it was already close to sunset and while I didn't see why we had to stop, I wasn't going to question my benefactor on the point; even though we should reach Albury in little time. Something about the world seemed strange, and I wasn't sure I could do anything about it.

"There's a pub 'long here a ways, we'll stop there tonight and yer can go ter Albury in the mornin'," she said.

Somehow, I assumed she meant together. She said it with the sort of tone that made you assume things. I didn't even question it. So I agreed. We travelled in silence for the next hour until the lights of a small town pub came into view. She pulled the car up and stopped, the engine still running. I was completely lost.

"Book a room 'n I'll park the car. Jus' ask fer a single."

My knees ached as I walked towards the entrance of the run-down old pub. Looking in the direction we were travelling, those stars were still in the same place. They flickered. The twins were watching me, and they weren't planning to go away.

Entering the building, I walked up to the bar, where a weathered sign hung, reading "Bookings and accommodation." The barman limped over.

"What can I do you for?"

Politely, I asked for a single room for the night. He looked past my shoulder out the door and shrugged and handed me a key.

"Room four. Up the stairs outside to the veranda, third door along."

She was waiting for me outside. The stars on the horizon seemed even brighter now. They still hadn't moved. The distant twins were haunting me, and it wasn't a feeling I enjoyed. We walked up the stairs in silence. She carried a plastic bag in one hand and a small, old sports bag in the other. Once inside, she handed me the plastic bag.

"You get tea on, while I clean up a bit."

There was a small bench in one corner with a few essentials, including a kettle and a microwave. Inside the bag were two frozen meals. They looked ancient, a brand I hadn't seen in the supermarket since I was a little kid. Oh well. I cracked them open and stuck them in the microwave.

As I turned, she was seated at a dresser across the room. Only a single dull lamp was on and I caught her face in the mirror. She appeared to be covered in blood, a jagged wound running diagonally the length of her face. A frantic, terrified look in those deep set, dark eyes. There was no sign of that lizard now.

"Are you okay?" I asked, taken aback.

She turned and her face was once again normal.

"Why wouldn' I be okay?" A puzzled expression lightened her face, removing any sign of the trouble I glimpsed a moment ago.

I shrugged it off as a trick of the light in the dully lit room.

Stepping outside, I lit a cigarette, taking a draw as I looked at the horizon. Those stars still lit up the sky in the same, strange place they had hung since I met her. Something was definitely odd about this evening, but I lacked the mental fortitude to question it, so I returned to the room, and to the strange girl I felt a peculiar kinship to.

Long into the night, we talked of everything. Life, love and loss. Anybody observing would have assumed us long-time lovers we were so comfortable together that night.

Later, after our fevered lovemaking in that hotel room in the middle of nowhere, I felt strangely liberated—muscles long tense were relaxed, both physically and metaphorically. My conscience was clear for the first time in a decade. I was forgiven, by myself as much as anybody else. Then in the morning, I awoke.

And I was alone. All my stuff was there: the frozen meal packet—wait, shouldn't there be two? My clothes, but only mine. My shoes by the door, my cigarette packet, half full but I thought she was smoking them too. None of *her* things were in the room at all. Only one empty glass stood on the sink, next to the rum bottle. Only one. That was odd, to say the least.

After getting dressed I went out onto the verandah. There was no sign of the car; no sign of her. And I still hadn't found out her name! In the dawn, the strangely placed stars had left, taking her with them.

Going downstairs, I entered the bar. The barman was cleaning. One solitary old man sat in a corner holding a schooner of dark beer. I walked over to the barman.

"Did you see where the girl I was with went?" I asked.

"What girl? You were alone," he said.

"She was right here. She picked me up after I rolled my car and brought me here. She was driving an old Gemini, she was in my room!"

"Sorry, no girl, no Gemini. You just walked in looking like a right mess and booked the room."

The old man had looked up, listening.

"Hey!" the old guy shouted, putting down his beer and waving a hand towards me. "What colour was that old Gemini?"

"Huh? Yellow," I replied. "It was pretty beaten up. It was a two door, the fast back. Might have been a nice car once."

"Damnit! That was my girl! You saw my girl! It has to be! Where were you headed?" He was getting insistent now.

Confused, I stammered, trying to think as the old man shook his hand at me.

"Al-Albury. I, I took a car and was heading to Albury to, to help a mate when I rolled it. She picked me up."

"No doubt about it, you saw my girl."

The man was getting excited. He stood, groaning, and lurched towards me.

"That was my girl! I've searched for her for so long! How come you saw my girl?"

The guy had to be pushing seventy. How could that fiery, delicious young woman be his girl? I asked him what he was talking about. He turned towards the door, signalling that I should follow him. Well, I had nothing better to do, since my ride was gone. So I followed.

We climbed into a beat up old four-wheel drive, and he started telling me a story. It was a story of his youth. A story thirty-four years old. He had been a young man then, he told me.

"As a young man, my best mate had been in Albury and had been stitched up. Arrested and charged for some crime he hadn't even committed," the old man told me.

He rambled for some time, trying to remember the facts of it all. I forget his exact words. Time had blurred the details but that was the essence. He had stolen a car, a yellow Gemini Coupe. It was brand new, from a car yard that'd had it proudly displayed right out the front, easily accessible to a desperate man.

"I took the car," the old man explained. "I dragged my girl along, headed off towards Albury to help my mate."

He paused for a long while as the old four by four rumbled along.

"The cops didn't want to let it go," he continued. "I crashed the Gemini. It ran off the road, out of control. The car rolled several times, for what seemed an eternity, before it came to rest. My girl was killed instantly."

79

As he told me his story, quiet tears streamed down the old man's face. When he was done, he sat in silence for a moment, before he spoke again.

"I was never able to love another woman," he said. "That day ruined me. All I ever worried about was her. From then on, I longed to know she was safe. That she had passed peacefully. I wanted her to be watching, smiling down on me. And felt she never was. Today, something feels different."

The old man was quiet for a few minutes after that, before he finally continued. "I was caught. They charged me with vehicular manslaughter, along with the theft, and a bunch of charges to do with running from police. I served twenty years for it. It wasn't enough. I loved that girl and I killed her."

The four-wheel drive turned off the road, bouncing over the lumpy ground, through the scrub, and then it came into view.

"They just left it here. The insurance company paid up and couldn't be bothered. The car yard had their money, so didn't care. It's a shrine to her now. A rusted, battered old shrine."

There it was. The beat-up old Gemini. The very same one I had ridden in the day before. My tears began forming, unbidden. He must have seen that.

"I never loved again. Not after that. You'd better have looked after her last night. I'm glad she found somebody to help her passing. She must've seen something of me in you. You get it, you understand, don't you?"

Numb, I nodded. Yes, I did understand. What he had said a short time earlier came back to me and I repeated it.

"Today, something feels different."

"That's right. I can move on with my life now. Thanks to you. Because she can move on, thanks to you."

There was much more than that. Maybe I had helped her out, but more so, she had saved me. Helped me. She'd taken me from that wreck and brought me here. She had stayed my hand; stopped my reckless run to Albury. I'd been saved by her; saved by a memory.

About the Author:

M. R. Mortimer is an Australian Fantasy and Science Fiction writer. He is a former teacher, and an Anthropologist, living in rural NSW. His available works include his Fantasy trilogy The Cinder Chronicles, *several stand-alone Science Fiction novels, and a short story collection. More information can be found on his website at **suspendedearth.com**.*

A Girl Called June

Nikky Lee

The schoolyard is half empty when Mum pulls into the pick-up zone. She glances at the swings, then the sandpit, hoping to see a familiar blond bob playing with the children there. The car door pops open.

"I made a friend today," Mya announces, wriggling into the backseat.

Mum beams. At last! "Oh? Who?"

Mya points to the air beside her. "Is it okay if she comes home to play?"

Another one. Mum's heart sinks. She forces a smile onto her face. She'll grow out of it, the psychologist had said. Just play along for now. "What's your friend's name?"

"June."

"That's a pretty name," Mum tells the air beside Mya.

Mya grins. "It's because her birthday is in June. Like mine!"

"Did June's parents say it's okay for her to visit?" Mum forces the words out.

Mya nods. "They're okay with it if you are."

She fights down a sigh. One friend. Was that asking too much? At seven Mya spent more time in her own head than with other children.

A nudge from the backseat. "So, can June come over?"

Their eyes meet in the rearview mirror.

"As long as you do your homework."

Mya woops and scurries across the backseat. "Come on," she urges, and after a pause, reaches over the vacant seat and pulls the door shut.

At home, Mum makes sandwiches. Peanut butter and jam.

"These are June's favourite too!" Mya says, engulfing one.

Don't be afraid to encourage her, Dr. Knowles had said. One day, it will be someone real. She pulls her thoughts together. "Seems you have a lot in common."

Mya shrugs and pencils an answer on her homework. "Of course we do, we're twins."

"I see."

Her daughter cocks her head, listening. "June says we were joined together once. Before the doctors pulled us apart."

Mum's stomach twists; her gaze drops to the long scar that ropes through Mya's hair, parting it in a circular incision. "Is that so?" Has Aaron said something to her?

"Don't worry Mum, June says the doctors didn't cut all of her away. That's why she's still here." Her face brightens. "Isn't that great? We can be a family." She turns to the empty chair beside her and her smile fades. "Except Grandpa."

Mum frowns. "Why not Grandpa?"

Mya's stares at space. Her face pales. "June says he's dead." Her lower lip trembles. "Is that true, Mum? Is Grandpa gone?"

"No, honey, Grandpa isn't gone. I spoke to him last night."

Mya wipes her eyes. "You're sure?"

"I'm sure."

Her daughter's relief is palpable.

Downstairs, the front door bangs: Dad returning home from work.

"Daddy!" Mya shoots up and races out the room, feet thumping down the stairs. "Daddy?"

"Ah, Mya." The moment he speaks, Mum knows something is wrong.

She races the last few steps. "Aaron, what—?"

"It's my Dad. He had an accident . . ."

Mum's stomach goes cold. "Mya, go upstairs."

"But Grandpa—"

"Now. Grandpa is fine. I told you." His eyes say the opposite.

With a long look, Mya retreats. Only when Mum hears the click of her bedroom door shutting does she speak.

"Really?"

Dad's face crumples.

"Oh, Aaron, I'm so sorry." She draws him into the lounge, sits him down, pats his shoulder. When he's calm, she asks, "Did you tell her about . . ?" She motions to her head, mirroring the scar in Mya's hair.

Dad stares at her, appalled. "No, never."

Mum shifts uncomfortably on the couch. "It's just today Mya said—"

"Mummy, Daddy." A weak voice echoes from the landing.

She rises. "What is it? Do you feel sick?"

"June says she's sorry."

Pandering to Mya's fantasy is the last thing she wants to do right now, but Mum sucks in a breath, forcing the smile again. "Why's that, honey?"

Mya gulps. "Because you're next, Mummy."

About the Author:

Nikky grew up as a barefoot 90s child in Perth, Western Australia, before moving to New Zealand in 2016. By day she works as a professional content writer and by night authors speculative fiction, often burning the candle at both ends to explore fantastic worlds, mine asteroids and meet wizards. Her creative work has appeared in magazines, on radio and in anthologies around the world. She is currently writing a dark fantasy trilogy, routinely sacrificing literary darlings to the editing gods in the hopes of seeing it published.

You can find her online at:
W:nikkythewriter.com | T:@NikkyMLee | F:nikkythewriter

THERE MUST ONLY BE ONE

Deeanna West

Blood and sweat mixed on the inside of her thighs, marring their creamy surface. She groaned again, exhaustion briefly overcoming the pain. Nine hours this had been going on for. Nine hours of contractions that seemed to tear her from deep inside and the incessant prattle of the nursemaids telling her just a few more pushes. If she'd had the strength, she would have strangled them. The Doctor said most Queens laboured for twelve hours before their heir escaped them. That meant three to go, not many in the scheme of things yet she didn't think she was going to make it. Darkness was already encroaching on the edge of her vision, threatening to drag her down into its depths.

"I see the head, my Queen, one last big push."

She obeyed, gritting her teeth and bearing down with what little remained of her energy.

With a gush of warm fluid, the baby was clear and fell into the waiting hands of the doctor. A high-pitched wail filled the room and had everyone within smiling. The princess was a strong one.

That should have been it. She should be able to breathe easier but still her abdomen clenched and sent pain shooting through her. Something was wrong. She screamed, loud despite her effort to smother it. An ache set into her fingers as she gripped the bed. The doctor turned back to her, face paling. In a swift motion, he placed the princess into the arms of one of the nurses and hurried back between her legs.

"I'm sorry, my Queen, but I need you to push again."

He didn't explain more than that, or at least, she didn't hear anything else. The pain was intense and she didn't know what was going on, but she trusted the doctor. Her efforts were feeble, but it must have been enough. In moments the doctor straightened, a second babe resting in his arms. She was the perfect mirror image of the first, the same thick mat of blonde hair upon her head. Only she was silent, staring at each person in the room as if committing their appearance to memory.

A nurse gasped but the others simply stared at the babe in horror.

"Show her to me," the Queen demanded, trying to push herself up in the bed.

The doctor hesitated but did as she bade, placing the child into her outstretched arms.

"Please, my Lady, there should only be one. We need to end this child's suffering now."

"No."

"Just her existence puts her sister's life in danger. There must only be one. You know the laws. She will doom us all."

"She is my daughter. She is a princess."

"She is not. Your firstborn is the princess, the only princess. She is the one that was meant to be. Focus on her, nurture her and Mercury will remain strong. Listen to me, your Majesty, let me take that one away and deal with it. Allowing it to live will only cause despair."

The Queen shook her head. She understood, of course. There was only ever one. But this child was her daughter too. She couldn't believe the girl was bad. Having two children was a blessing no Queen before her had received. She would not let one of them be murdered in the name of superstition.

"Doctor, the twins are to be protected. I'm sure their birth marks a great time for our people."

He nodded, taking the child and placing her in the cot beside her sister. They were beautiful, a matching pair with their soft blonde hair and intense green eyes.

The sharp tang of burning flesh filled the room, overpowering the disinfectants that usually claimed top spot. I couldn't help but hesitate before pushing further into the room. They had told me what happened, the attack and how many men we lost, but being prepared for something wasn't the same as actually seeing it. Gritting my teeth, I rushed to the first bed. The plastic hospital sheets were soiled with blood and ash, but I couldn't focus on that.

Deep rents cut through flesh and bone left his limbs limp. His chest struggled to rise, stuttering and gasping with each breath. Blood from a gash in his side splattered the blanket with each movement he made. He would die soon, there was no doubt about that. I could almost see the sepsis spreading through his veins, wrapping its darkness around his heart and squeezing tight. My fingers itched, desperate to touch him, to sink into his flesh and pull him back to the light.

Carefully, I selected an area unmarred by injury and placed my palms to him. Heat flowed into me as soon I touched his skin. Already he fevered. I needed to hurry. Closing my eyes, I sent my magic loose. It sunk through our point of contact and burnt through his body. As if watching from afar, I saw his body thrash, heard his groans as bones cracked back into place and scrunched my nose as he released his bowels.

No one ever said healing was pretty.

Hours later, at least it felt like hours, though it almost never was, I felt the last vessel knit back together. I released my contact, separating myself from him in a rush of weakness that dropped me to my knees.

"Your Highness, are you alright?"

"It's fine," I replied, trying to force my breathing into more even beats and keep the annoyance out of my voice. The doctor had served us since long before I was born, he'd seen my abilities develop so he knew I was always tired afterward. It would pass, he didn't need to treat me like a child. I accepted his hand anyway and allowed him to pull me to my feet.

"Maybe you should sit?" he continued, trying to force me into a chair.

"I'm okay, Haavard." I needed to check the man, make sure I had completed his healing.

"Please your Highness . . ."

"Giselle."

"I can't."

"You can. Haavard, you know I prefer my name to royal titles I am yet to earn."

The moment he sighed I knew I had won. He'd follow my instruction for a few days and then we'd have the argument once again. That was the nature of our relationship. No matter how many mangled bodies we shared, he still couldn't bring himself to be familiar.

Turning my attention back to the man, I couldn't help but smile. He was perfect. Not a blemish marked his body let alone an injury. One of the nurses met my eye and smiled back at me.

"Thank you, Your Highness . . . Giselle. Your power is inspirational."

I nodded my acknowledgement and headed for the door. I'd heard it before, the coos of platitudes flung at me when I was within earshot. *'You will be the most powerful Queen.' 'Your healing is stronger than your mother's ever was.' 'No queen has ever been able to bring people back from the brink of death.'*

I would accept them more readily if I didn't know the darker comments that were flitting through the hallways. The laments and the hate that circled everywhere across the planet. Every compliment followed by, *'Too bad she is destined for despair, too bad she was cursed the moment her sister took breath.'* Some even had the audacity to whisper the downfall of Murcurian monarchy. Insanity, that's what it was, but it had haunted Gianna and I our entire lives.

It was getting harder to bite down the bitterness, but I'd show them, eventually. When coronation day came, they would realise the fact I had a sister was not a bad omen. I had to think of something else.

"How did the Teriack get so close?" I asked Cassian.

I didn't have to turn to know he was there. He had been my shadow for years. Protector, confidant, whatever name you gave him, he was practically an extension of myself. Always there.

"I cannot be sure, but they appeared to know our scouts' flight paths."

"Those patterns are changed daily."

"I am aware." He practically snapped but it didn't matter. He could talk to me any way he pleased. I'd descend into madness if he started bowing and scraping and calling me 'Highness'.

He sighed, running his hand through his hair in frustration. I had to fight not to laugh as the dark strands stayed on end.

"Tell me what you're thinking, Cassian. I need all the information I can get if I'm to stand with mother on the council tomorrow."

"Only the Commanding Officer of each fleet are aware of the flight paths ahead of schedule. The pilots themselves only receive their orders in the moments before launch. The Teriack had to receive the information from the C.O.'s."

I nodded. I knew how the flights were organised as well as anyone, so it wasn't a surprise. Well, the fact that we may have a Teriack sympathiser within the palace was a little shocking. "A little detour is in order, I think. Let's go visit this morning's C.O."

Cassian didn't respond, he'd probably had the same thought after all. He led me down the endless marble corridors of the palace, spiraling to the lower levels where the military were housed. I didn't venture down here often. Usually injured soldiers were raced straight to the med bay and I met them there.

"He'll be at the monitors still. The fighters are driving off the last of the Teriack."

It made sense. We descended into a small control room, the walls lined with monitors, maps and stratagem. Cassian was right, the C.O. was there.

He had been dead for hours. I gagged as the smell assaulted us. His bowels had released when he died, and the odour had accumulated from the hours spent in the enclosed room. Rigor mortis had already caused his limbs to splay out stiffly at his side. I had seen dead bodies of course, but these had died on the table faster than I could heal them.

Cassian moved closer to the body, searching for any sign of what had killed him, going as far as rolling him over with his foot. "Nothing," he stated.

I believed him but it didn't make sense. Healthy men didn't just drop dead and with the leaked information . . .

I moved close to look for myself but there really was nothing. Not a mark marred his skin. "Could it be suicide?" I mused. "Poison or something else that wouldn't leave an obvious trace? A guilty conscience after working with the Teriack?"

Cassian stared at me thoughtfully before replying. "Maybe," he finally admitted. "But why? If someone was going to betray us to the

Teriack, it would be for some sort of gain. Why kill yourself and not enjoy whatever you were getting out of the deal?"

"It's certainly strange. Supervise Haavard's autopsy, would you? I don't want anyone left alone with the body until he's finished. I'll report to Mother."

I found Mother in the throne room, draped upon the great marble atrocity with a grace I could never hope to emulate. As children, Gianna and I would climb onto the throne and imagine we were legendary Queens, all-powerful twins ready to conquer the universe. Until the advisors found us. They dragged Gianna off, hissing at her for leaving her taint upon such an important thing as the throne. Despite my protests, they had banned her from the room. I had even demanded, on order of the princess and with all the dignity and shrillness of an eight-year-old, but it had made no difference. Mother had tried to end such horrid thinking but so many of her people thought so strongly against Gianna that she'd had to concede some things just to keep the peace. She certainly had a hard life, my sister.

The room hadn't changed much since that day. The same glowing golden banners hung upon the walls amongst the tapestries and the same attendants stood guarding the entries.

"Mother, we have a problem," I called as soon as I entered. There was no point rambling pleasantries. We had defeated this fleet of Teriack but who knew how many more were out there waiting. And now a murder, or suicide, or whatever. No, certainly no time to chat.

THERE MUST ONLY BE ONE

Mother raised a perfectly tweezed eyebrow but didn't reply, clearly waiting for me to continue. In a rush I told her what had happened, ending in a gasp from not breathing enough. It was a relief to tell her, she could take care of this mess now. I was built for healing. My magic had effectively ended accidental deaths after all. I wasn't meant to be running around the halls sprouting theories on murders like some kind of amateur detective. Yes, this would be better. Mother would send out her enquiries and fix everything. We would drive the Teriack away once again.

"You've always had an overactive imagination, Giselle."

She may as well have punched me in the stomach. I didn't drop to my knees like I wanted to, but suddenly it was a struggle to breath. She didn't believe me.

"Mother, you can see the body. I'm not making this up."

"Oh, I don't doubt there is a body. It's a shame whenever we lose someone, and I understand you must feel guilty for not being able to heal him. But making the man a villain will not ease your own shortcomings. You are to be Queen, Giselle."

I couldn't believe what I was hearing. Mother had always been tough. While she didn't believe Gianna was a curse to my reign, she still forced me to work harder and harder. I forced my tone to remain even. "Mother the—"

"You need to be better, Giselle. Stronger. Despite your coronation being only a month away, you're still lacking the qualities you need to be Queen."

Her words hurt. I had healed so many people, yet it still wasn't enough. Salt burned my eyes from the tears gathering there. I tried to blink them away, but my hands clenched at my sides and I felt the wetness on my cheeks. If she saw me crying, I'd never hear the end of it. I turned on my heel, keeping my stride short of running and escaped the room.

"I don't know why you keep trying to impress her."

Gianna's voice was flat. She wasn't the sort to scream and rage. No, when Gianna was angry, her voice became more even, not exactly a monotone but the inflections within her words were bitten off the angrier she became.

She began to pace. "For pity's sake, Giselle, you are the princess, you will be the next Queen whether she likes it or not. I hate to sound like Mother, but you need to start acting like it. The woman is a menace, ignore her."

The criticism didn't seem as harsh coming from her and I nodded.

"I know, Gi, I just keep waiting for some glimpse of who she used to be. The woman that sacrificed everything to keep you alive. That woman wouldn't have done that if she didn't love us, right?"

"I'm sure she loved the idea of two daughters. Of being the only Queen to birth twins. But I fear the reality has fallen short of her expectations. And it doesn't help that everyone is constantly whispering about what a curse I am. Questioning why she would let a harbinger of despair live."

Gianna threw herself down on the bed beside me with a humph. I didn't need to see it to know her hair would be mixing with mine, the exact same golden hue. We were the perfect pair and despite Gianna not being the heir, I was determined we would rule together.

I rolled onto my stomach to look at her. "Don't talk about it. You know you're not some monster. People are idiots. You're stronger than I ever could be. You should be the Queen."

Something flashed in her eyes, something I didn't recognise, but then she was laughing and it was gone. "You're the idiot. I don't even have magic. What kind of Queen would that make me?"

"Oh, I can see it now," I teased. Gianna rarely laughed so now that she was, I was loath to let her joy fade again. "They will parade you down the streets shouting 'all hail Queen Gianna, the breaker of magics and liberator of Mercury'."

"What am I liberating them from?"

"Mother?" I suggested.

She laughed again, a deep laugh I hadn't heard for months. Gasping, she clutched at her sides. "Yes, I like that."

Shadows obscured my view of the room. The corners steeped in so much darkness it was impossible to see what they contained. It didn't matter though. Tonight, the shadows were my friend, my cloak of protection to prevent anyone from seeing me. There was only one death scheduled and while I would relish destroying anyone who saw me, it wasn't the time. Yes, a single death would be better, more poignant somehow. I crept through the room silently, careful not to knock a foot against a chair and give myself away. I didn't need to surprise her. Even if she saw me coming, it'd only take a touch. I

paused in the next doorway. She looked like a simple, darker area in this light. Nothing more than a sleeping figure, she could be anyone. Nothing marked her as Queen. I smiled and stepped forward. She would die like anyone else too.

She didn't wake until my hand clasped around her throat. Her eyes flicked open, recognition and then panic flitting across them. I didn't give her a chance to speak. Black tendrils sunk into her body where my hands met her skin. Oily fingers that wrapped around her windpipe, stopping her from crying out and forcing her to gasp for what little breath she could. Her eyes bulged. She knew why she was dying, and I was glad.

The blackness of my magic crawled through her body. It wasn't fast. I hadn't mastered controlling its speed yet. But it encased each organ it came to, squeezing the life from her until finally, she spasmed and died.

I stared down at her for a moment. No wounds marked her passing, her face was still that of the Queen's. How disappointing. I smiled anyway. The body may not show it, but I knew death by my magic was painful. Turning, I slunk back into the night. I was done for the moment, but there was one to go. One more person standing in my way.

Screams. They dragged me kicking and screaming from sleep, yet it still took a moment before my wits returned. The voices sounded right outside my chambers but the only person who should be there was my maid. It had been warm when I had retired, so the shift I wore was thin, not sheer but it clung to my body regardless. I hesitated until the sound of tears falling took the place of the shouts. Impropriety be damned. I flung open the door to find my maid wrapped in the arms of a guard. Some recollection of their relationship spun through my mind.

"Limara, what's wrong?"

Her man glanced up at my words, pink blush spreading across his cheeks as he realised my state of undress before quickly turning his gaze away again. She hiccupped, trying to get her sobs under control. I didn't rush her, something had clearly shaken her to the core. Finally, she wiped the tears from her eyes and turned her attention to me fully, though she still clung to the man's hand. "Oh, Giselle, I'm sorry, I'm so very sorry."

The iron grip of fear clenched my stomach. "What's going on?"

Another round of tears sprung fresh to her eyes, forcing Limara into the man's chest once more. He wrapped his arms around her and replied on her behalf. "It's the Queen. She's dead."

Shock sent my feet moving before I even registered his words. I ran towards Mother's chambers, heedless of the chill seeping into my bare feet. I didn't have far to go. Her rooms were in the same wing of the palace as mine and Gianna's.

Haavard and Gianna were already there. The doctor held Gianna back as tears streamed down her cheeks and she fought to approach the body of her mother. I had no tears. It didn't make sense. It was like I was one of the automatons that mined the asteroids. By all reasoning I should be the one collapsing in Haavard's arms. I had certainly cared for mother more than Gianna ever seemed to. But there was nothing in me. The space where my emotions lived had frozen into numbness.

She looked like she was sleeping. Still beneath the covers no matter how I stared, waiting for the blankets to rise with her breath. Like the officer, she had no wounds that I could see, no logical reason for her death.

"Haavard, what happened here?" My voice sounded hollow even to my own ears, but I ignored the concerned look he sent my way.

"Her maid found her like this when she came to awaken her for the day. Nothing has been touched, my Queen."

His formalness almost cracked through my numbness. The line of succession was clear, Mother was dead, and now I was expected to be Queen. At least, acting Queen until my coronation. All the responsibility of the monarchy was suddenly on my shoulders and I wasn't ready. Fear clawed its way past my walls and it took all my strength to swallow and stride closer to the bed.

"I want you to examine her here, Haavard. This was not a natural death, I'm sure of it. Examine her and find something I can use to catch whoever did this. You have two bodies now, there are no excuses."

He nodded, cautiously letting go of Gianna to speak in hushed tones to the guards outside the room. I grabbed Gianna's arm, pulling her after me as I returned to my room. As I closed the door, she sunk onto the bed.

"Giselle, what's going on?" she whispered, clearly in shock but at least the tears had dried. She knew about the officer, of course, but the question came more from grief than an actual lack of understanding. I joined her on the bed and wrapped her into a hug.

THERE MUST ONLY BE ONE

We sat there, seeking comfort in each other's embrace until finally, our stomachs demanded we break our fast and we were forced to return again to the world. I would have to plan Mother's funeral as well, but I didn't discuss that with Gianna. Let her grieve without the stress of that to plague her for now.

Peace. Finally. I let myself sink to the floor, heedless of the sleeping man on the gurney I had just healed. My head swam and hunger gnawed at me with a ferocity I had never known. Cassian and Haavard had been forcing food in my direction but I was spent. The Teriack were relentless, launching more and more attacks until I was healing so much it didn't matter how much I ate. My energy levels just weren't getting a chance to replenish. It was clear now, the Teriack knew our movements, could counter any stratagem we employed against them. We were hanging on by the sheer force of will and I doubted how long we would last. Between the healings and searching for our still at large murderer, poor Mother's funeral had taken the back seat. Oh, it had been a lavish affair, of course, but not as large as a Queen deserved. I had thought Gianna would have stepped up to help with it. We were grieving together after all and I was doing everything else, but she never offered. When I pushed the issue and asked for help, it had not been a good conversation. She had screamed at me then disappeared for two days. She was so aloof. All I wanted was to hug her and have her stand beside me but clearly that wasn't going to happen. I didn't have time to dwell. Haavard had asked me to meet him after all.

Leaving the med bay, I headed towards his chambers. Why he wanted to meet me there I had no idea. His rooms were dark, no light escaping beneath the door to mark his presence within. Confusion flared but I knocked anyway. The door cracked open in response, barely wide enough for a hand to snake out and drag me inside.

"Haavard, what in the universe?" I gasped as the door snapped shut behind me.

"I'm sorry, my Queen. But I need to ask you something."

"I've not been coronated yet, and why does it require us to be in the dark?"

"I don't think you'll want anyone to overhear what I'm about to ask."

I squinted at him in the gloom. Haavard had been old for as long as I could remember. He was a funny old man, crotchety at the best of times although Mother claimed he had been more joyful when he was younger. Or at least before she had let Gianna live against his wishes. I loved him like a grandparent but there had always been some layer of mistrust between us, I couldn't forgive him for trying to kill my sister.

"What is it Haavard?"

"I hope you can forgive me, but I must ask," he whispered, wringing his hands and pausing before continuing in a gush of breath. "These murders. There are no marks upon the bodies and yet it appears like their organs have all given out. The internal strain is catastrophic, crushed kidneys, torn cardiac valves and the like with no reason for it to happen. They died as if by magic."

My stomach clenched as I realised what he was insinuating, and I couldn't help my mouth dropping open in shock that he would even consider it.

"Your magic, my Queen," he continued. "It manipulates the body, forcing it to heal faster than normal and against wounds it usually would not be able to recover from. You could use it to stop a heart as easily as start one."

He said it. I couldn't believe he said it. Indignation burned across my face. "How dare you," I hissed. "I heal, my magic heals, it does not kill. You may not be able to comprehend this, but healing magic is a pure force. Even if I wanted to, which I never have, I would not be able to use it to kill."

He had the decency to look ashamed. My anger faded. He hadn't wanted to ask, hadn't wanted to doubt me and I could see that. He was as stressed by the situation as I was.

"It's okay," I conceded. "I'm frustrated too."

He nodded. "I'm sorry my Queen. I have examined the bodies and I just can't find another explanation."

"Magic."

"Yes. Anything short of that would have left a mark on the skin."

We stared at each other in the darkness, pondering the dilemma in front of us. I think we realised at the same time. Horror dawned in his eyes and I'm sure it was matched in my own. She was my mirror image, everyone said so.

"Gianna," I breathed. I launched towards the door, flinging it wide to barrel down the corridor.

"My Queen, wait!" Haavard's voice chased me down the hall but I couldn't wait, couldn't stop even though I could hear him chasing after me. He wouldn't catch me.

I knew the truth now, but I had to confront her, had to hear it from her lips. Everyone had been right. Evil they had called her, filled with darkness, despair bringer and I had defended her at every turn. How stupid I had been.

She was in the shuttle bays, standing in front of the controls. She turned at the sound of my arrival. She smiled.

"So, you've worked it out." Her voice was flat and cold. The same voice she used when angry but now I understood, this was her real self. The rest had all been an act.

I wanted to ask so much. Scream at her and demand an explanation for the officer, for Mother and for the Teriack for surely it had been her to betray us to them as well.

"Why?"

She grinned again, fingers caressing the console in front of her. "Why not?"

It wasn't the answer I was expecting. Her life had been hard, I knew that, but I thought she was strong enough to not let it bother her. That she was ready to stand beside me once I was Queen. If anything, I thought she'd say that she resented me or something and wanted the monarchy all to herself. To be so unfeeling about the horror she had wrought, she was insane.

"How could you, Gianna? We were going to rule together."

"Together?" she spat. "Don't be a fool, Giselle. You know the adage as well as me. There must only be one. In some sick twist of fate you are that one, but I'm not going to have it. I am so much stronger than you."

"You killed Mother."

"Oh yes, that was easy. You see, dear sister, my magic may have taken longer to reveal itself, but it is everything yours is not. Healing someone is nothing. I am death, with a single touch I can send someone into oblivion."

"No."

"Yes. But I'm bored. You bore me, always have. So, I'm afraid it's time to say goodbye." She flicked a switch on the console and instantly the doors of the hangar opened. They had clearly been waiting. The Teriack swarmed through the opening, ray guns armed and ready. They paused beside Gianna, clearly under her command.

"Sorry, sis." She shrugged and strode forward, hand reaching for me. I scrambled backwards, not quite realising what she was intending to do.

Haavard and Cassian burst into the room behind me. Dimly, I recognised Haavard must have sought out Cassian for help.

"No!"

Cassian's shout was everything, his movements demanding all my attention until the room seemed stuck in slow motion. He threw himself in front of me, blocking me from Gianna even as he shoved me backwards. I fell into Haavard's arms, fighting as he tried to drag me out of the room. Caasian's body crumped as if Gianna's touch had stolen his bones; he hit the ground hard. My screams split the air at the same time the gunfire did.

"We must go!" Haavard shouted, tugging at my arm.

I couldn't think, all I could see was Cassian falling over and over again overshadowed with the pleasure in Gianna's eyes. Numbness took control until my muscles followed Haavard automatically. Scorch marks flared on the walls as the gunfire collided with the marble. Haavard led me in a zigzag, racing as fast as his arthritic legs would carry him until we burst into Mother's chambers. He slammed the door behind us, and I helped him drag a dresser in front of it.

"We need to hurry." His breath was coming in ragged gasps now, but he didn't stop to catch it. Again, he grabbed my hand and led me to the wall behind the great royal bed. There, behind a tapestry was a small door. I hadn't known it was there. The tapestry was one that had hung beside the bed for as long as I could remember. The rich colours of its weaving long since faded with time.

"What is this?" I couldn't help but ask.

"Our escape," he grunted, not explaining further as he pulled open the door.

The room beyond was small, nothing like the grandeur of the royal chambers. It didn't have to be. The only item within was a shuttle. Small, only designed to transport two, maybe three people at a push. Despite that it was sleek, all shining metal and chrome.

Pounding on the door, he drove us forward into the shuttle. With a hiss the hatch sealed, enclosing us within as the Teriack forced their way through. Haavard didn't hesitate. Yanking on the throttle we launched out of the palace and into the sky. Shots followed us but we rapidly left their range. Gianna stood on the secret launch pad, staring up at us with cold eyes full of hate . . .

Haavard's piloting was not smooth. We shot forward only to slam to a stop seconds later. It was jarring and nausea rolled in my gut, but

106

I said nothing, I lacked the strength. I sat there, slumped in my seat as we broke the atmosphere, Gianna's laughter chasing us the entire way.

Only a heartbeat later, the dark expanse of space stretched out before us. A stunning view, but I couldn't appreciate it. My eyes stayed fixed on the planet disappearing behind us. A glowing globe of regret. Gianna's laugh echoed within my mind. I would never forget that sound. I would replay it, over and over to fuel my anger, to sustain it until I was face to face with her again. The day would come when I saw her again and I would end her. There could only be one. I'd heard it all my life, had doubted it but Gianna had proved it right. There could only be one and I would make sure that it was me.

About the Author:

Deeanna West is a fantasy author writing from sunny north Queensland. If a book has magic, strange and amazing creatures or a world completely different to our own, then she's sold. When not holed up writing, she can be found playing games on the Xbox or out riding her horse.

THE FAKTOR INCIDENT

Aiki Flinthart

This is a prequel to IRON, first in the *Kalima Chronicles* trilogy.
The Faktor Incident is set 2 years before IRON.

"I'm not entirely sure what to do with you, Pellar." The Weishi
House Master, Hao, drummed lean fingers on his zitan-wood desk.
He tugged at his long goatee and straggly moustache.

Pell waited silently, gripping his bronze dagger and poison-dart
belt, weight balanced for movement.

In the snowy street outside, merchants hawked their wares and
wagons rattled past Weishi House. A Messenger House runner
bolted down the street and yelled fresh news: Prince Soran's eldest
child would be invested as heir at midday the next day.

Master Hao harrumphed and gestured at the straight-backed
visitor's chair. "Sit, Pellar."

"I prefer Pell, sir." He remained standing. One never knew, in Weishi House, when a master would launch a surprise attack. Best to stay ready. He'd survived eighteen years by being on his guard.

Master Hao sent him a sharp look and didn't reply.

Nearby, Merchant House's timekeeper bells tolled the midday hour. Master Hao rolled his eyes and waited. Pell stayed silent, unmoving.

More bells pealed throughout the snowy valley that sheltered Nanqualea town, capital of the Princedom of Jadid. A deeper bell chimed in from Prince Soran Salib's hill keep.

Finally, the ringtones faded.

"Right, Pellar." Master Hao cleared his throat and shuffled a pile of bamboo paper on his desk. "This is a high-level assassination. Not often given to an unbearded new graduate xiongshou. Even one with the House record for concealment and the best 'assassinations' of every House master." He looked up, narrow-eyed. "But it's approved by Xintou House. And the person who paid for this contract asked for you, specifically."

"Sir?" Pell repeated. Outside Weishi House, very few people even knew he existed. He'd been given to the House as a nameless infant. Not even a family tattoo on his forearm. Unable to walk freely about the city without that tattoo. Stuck in the House. Raised by the masters and the older boys.

He tightened his grip on his dagger. With the ease of long practice, Pell shunted aside the more . . . unpleasant memories of what that 'raising' entailed.

Never again.

"Are you willing to undertake this task?" Master Hao asked.

"I need more detail, sir. Who authorised it?"

Hao sighed and swiped a hand over his shortcut hair. "Mistress Xiaan—Prince Soran's Bonded Xintou—signed the contract. But she's refused to reveal who paid for it." He spread his hands. "How can I say no to a Bonded Xintou?"

Pell said nothing to what was probably a rhetorical question. He suppressed a shiver. Any of the Xintou House telepathic women made him uneasy. A Bonded Xintou attached to the Prince was even more frightening. He had learned to ward his mind—as all xiongshou must. But he was a non-telepath. Unable to tell if his wards were penetrated. The thought of the Prince's gold-veiled, gold-robed, Bonded Xintou rummaging about in his head made his stomach churn.

He struggled to keep his expression bland.

Master Hao stared at the papers on his desk and muttered, "I suppose it shouldn't surprise us that Mistress Xiaan approved the death of a noble." He smiled thinly. "After all, eighteen years ago Xintou House agreed to the anti-kin-child laws and the murder of thousands of children."

Pell clenched his teeth. So many Jadid children had been murdered just they lacked their father's family tattoo. Was that Pell's mother's excuse for hiding him here; imprisoning him? Had she feared he would be murdered by the blood-crazed mobs that had swept Kalima and Jadid eighteen years ago?

Why had Xintou House allowed it? Why had they pilloried single mothers, when xintou were guilty of the same crime? After all, xintou could manipulate DNA and create children in their own image. And xintou were forbidden to birth twins or boys for fear of causing some long-forgotten defect.

So, perhaps Xintou House condemned unwed common women and untattooed children out of jealousy or spite? Pell pressed his lips thin. There was no other logic behind the kin-child massacres.

With a heavy sigh, Master Hao slid the topmost sheet of paper toward Pell. "Take the contract, boy. But, when you're done, get out of Nanqualea. This town isn't big enough, no matter how skilled you are at hiding. I've never met your target, but he's well-enough liked. You won't be popular with the younger generation if the news of who took the contract leaks. Legal or not, it could make you a target for revenge attacks."

Pell lifted his brows. Weishi House didn't accept contracts on their own people.

"Don't worry, boy." Hao's mouth twisted. "I wouldn't authorise a kill on you. But that won't stop an angry mob of commoners."

Unfolding the contract, Pell said nothing until he read the target's name.

Then he allowed surprise to show. "Truly?"

"Yes," Hao replied. "Yes, indeed. While I don't want you to fail—for the sake of your career—I very much do want you to fail. If you understand my meaning."

Pell swallowed, folded the contract into a perfect square and tucked it into a pocket in his black weishi uniform. His hands trembled, just a fraction. He controlled himself, quashing the tremor low in his stomach. Excitement, that was what it was. After all, this was what he'd trained for since he was three. There was no place for hesitation or doubt in a xiongshou's mind.

Bowing, Pell turned away.

"Wait!" Hao opened a drawer. "We'll forego the usual graduation and manhood ceremony for the sake of anonymity." He rose and spoke more formally, "By the skill shown during the last three weeks of your assessment, I grant you the rank of xiongshou, with all the privileges and responsibilities inherent in that."

He tossed a scrap of cloth across the desk. "Here. Take this with my blessing. You'll have to cut your own hair and let your beard grow." His frown gentled. "You've been a model student, Pell. I know it hasn't always been easy here, but you're a good lad. I see that in you. The tattooist is waiting to put the House shuriken tattoo on your wrist. Do me proud. Then get out of here and don't come back for at least five years."

Slowly, Pell picked up the black and purple braided silk bracelet. He tightened it around his wrist. The bracelet would grant admission into any Weishi House in any country. It also meant he could kill any target.

Assuming he had a contract authorised by the Xintou House Law Mistresses and a Weishi House.

A smouldering coal, deep in his gut, flared into fire. He'd worked for fifteen years to attain the bracelet. To have it tossed at him like a scrap of rubbish; to have to cut his own hair short for manhood . . . It seemed . . . unfitting.

Outside the window, heavy storm clouds had finally lifted, revealing a peridot sky for the first time in the long winter months. Bowing once more, Pell left Hao's office without a backward look.

His childhood was over.

"Faktor? Where *is* that boy?" A deep, raspy voice echoed through chill hallways.

Pell slowed his breathing and focussed on stillness. Yelling, Prince Soran Salib, passed beneath Pell's position. Soran wore the leather kilt and open, blood-red robe that was the traditional men's garb in Jadid. His heavy footfalls slapped back from the great hill keep's thick walls.

Pale orange sunlight slanted through a narrow window and glinted off the pendant on Soran's thickly-pelted chest. The symbol of office for the ruling Prince of Jadid; a silver-metal lion's head. Not the more rare and valuable iron, if Pell was any judge. Jadid had no iron mines. Very few existed anywhere on the planet of Kalima.

Prince Soran paused in the hall.

Pell held his breath. If he failed this, he would have to go back to ordinary weishi work. Bodyguarding for rich merchants and nobles. If he succeeded, Jadid could be thrown into turmoil for years to come.

He gave a wintry smile.

Failure wasn't an option. He would complete the contract and get out of this foresaken country. Take assignments in other cities. Travel and see the rest of Kalima. Somewhere warmer than the Princedom of Jadid with its endless dour winters, dismal timber cutters, and snow deer farmers.

He caught his straying thoughts and dragged them back to here-and-now. A xiongshou couldn't lose concentration. Even for a second.

Mistress Xiaan rounded the corner, resplendent and terrifying in her shimmering gold silk robes. The corners of her mouth were pulled down, clearly visible below the translucent gold veil that hid her eyes.

"Faktor's nowhere, Shenshi Soran. That unbearded boy has managed to hide from us for three full days. He can't miss his investiture as your heir. It's his birthright. His responsibility."

Soran snorted. "The boy thinks of nothing but books and ancient history. The boy talks gibberish. He needs to understand politics and economics. Deal with living people, not the long-dead fools that founded this deserted colony-world." He ran restless fingers through his full, dark beard.

Xiaan laid a hand on Soran's massive forearm, her thin fingers pale against his swarthy skin and his faded blue lion's-head family tattoo.

The new black shuriken inked onto Pell's arm was still raised and red. Solitary without a family tattoo. He resisted the urge to scratch, and lay flat atop a tall yar-pine cupboard that stood in the corridor.

"We'll find Faktor," Xiaan said soothingly.

"I don't have any more time to waste," Soran snarled. "That trouble-maker, Corin Mal-kin, is here as emissary from the northern Jun Second, Rafi Koh-Lin. I don't trust that Mal-kin character. Too flippant for my liking. Never takes anything seriously."

The Xintou's thin mouth curved into a smile. "Corin Mal-kin means no harm, shenshi. Devious, I grant you, but I've Read his thoughts enough to know his intentions are good. Just don't leave him alone with your daughter or your purse."

Pell grinned. Mal-kin sounded like an interesting man. Perhaps someone who might offer passage out of Jadid when this contract was completed.

"Well," Soran said, sighing, "Mal-kin's disappeared somewhere as well. My weishi-guards lost sight of him in the city and that worries me."

Mistress Xiaan chewed on her lip. "That is somewhat concerning. But he's due to leave Jadid tomorrow afternoon."

With a gruff laugh, Soran patted Mistress Xiaan's wrist. "Don't mind me. Just find Faktor. We have twelve hours before the investiture. In an hour I have to meet with Mal-kin about that new trade deal. I'm sure he'll show up. But if he wants our yar-pine he can jiche-well pay for it this time. I want grain and a lot of it."

"I'll find Faktor." Mistress Xiaan bowed. "I can sense he's still here in the keep. But he's adept at hiding, so I can't pin down where."

From his place above their line of sight, Pell allowed himself a small smile and strengthened his own mental wards. He'd snuck through this keep many times in the last six months. Training; learning to steal unseen to and from the most heavily-guarded building in the city. He probably knew the keep better than Soran did.

Since Soran's people must have searched every room, there was only one place Faktor could be.

A third person joined Soran and Xiaan. Yarina, Soran's sixteen-year-old daughter. Faktor's younger half-sister. Darkly pretty with flashing eyes and a confidant way of throwing her shoulders back and lifting her chin.

116

"Did you find him?" she demanded, folding her arms across her lilac silk robe.

Soran rubbed at his forehead. "No, daughter. Go back to your studies and leave your brother to me. He'll be there."

Her lips pursed. "When will you get it into your head, Father? Faktor doesn't want to be heir. Forcing him won't make him a good ruler for Jadid."

Soran said nothing, his heavy lids drooping. This looked like an old argument he couldn't be bothered fighting any more.

Yarina made a noise of frustration and stalked off, her hands clenched at her sides.

"I need to find that girl a husband," Soran muttered.

"I don't know that's what *she* needs, shenshi." Xiaan chuckled, low in her throat.

He gestured irritably. "Go find Faktor. Meet me and Corin Malkin, later, in the conference room."

She bowed and strode away on silent, gold-slippered feet. Soran watched her out of sight, an old, aching regret in his eyes. Then he shook his head and stomped toward the great hall.

Pell waited a few minutes and dropped soundlessly to the floor, dusting off his dark clothing. He glanced up and down the hall. Then he pressed a decorative knob on the cupboard and heaved the timber frame away from the wall. The hinges opened soundlessly. Someone had oiled the door recently, leaving a whiff of mel-oil hanging in the air.

Once inside, the secret door swung easily shut and Pell waited for his eyes to adjust to the semi-gloom. No footprints on the stone floor. The narrow hall's floor was swept clean. Soft-shoed, Pell crept toward the far door. His heart skittered and jumped, his breathing quickening. He took three slow, deep breaths to control himself.

The thick wooden door opened silently. Pell peered around, checking for threats and exits. Only a comfortable sitting room was visible. Half-shadowed in darkness. Pell totted up the room's contents. Just one mel-oil lantern pooled light in a sheltered corner. Two faded armchairs, a threadbare rug, and a battered yar-pine desk. Stacked on the desk stood a dozen thick books.

At the desk sat young man, his attention focussed on an open book. The young man's face was only half-visible, but faintly familiar.

Faktor. The intended heir.

And the intended victim whose name lay on Pell's authorised contract.

Could it be this easy? Pell hesitated. No weishi-guards were in sight. Yes. This was the best chance he had to complete the contract.

He slipped into the room, with blowpipe ready and a grey-feathered dart in the tube. A quiet breath of dust-thickened air and he pressed the tube to his lips. One quick blow. Silent. Accurate.

The dart embedded in the young man's neck.

Faktor jumped to his feet, tipping his chair over. He gargled and scrabbled at the dart. Yanking it out, he gazed at the dart, then wide-eyed at Pell.

Pell strode forward and murmured the xiongshou's traditional last words to a victim, "My respects to your ancestors."

Faktor gave a gurgling sigh and collapsed, eyes rolled up. The dart fell from his fingers and tinkled on the stone floor.

"What the . . ." A new voice intruded. Male, sharp, deep.

THE FAKTOR INCIDENT

Snatching his bronze dagger from his hip, Pell spun to face the threat. A tall man emerged through a second doorway. Pell cursed himself for stupidity. He hadn't cleared the room properly. How could he be so amateur?

The main door was too far for an easy escape. Pell held his position, keeping his back to the one mel-oil lamp. Hopefully the semi-darkness would protect him. He dropped into a fighting stance, bronze dagger ready. The man's startling green eyes glittered, one hand on his sword pommel.

"What have you done?" the man demanded, pointing at the body lying on the floor. "That's the heir to Jadid." His eyes flickered to Pell's wrist and he hesitated, frowning. "You're a xiongshou? Show me your contract."

Pell raised both hands. He could only kill someone who interfered with his task. But this contract was fulfilled. Now someone had demanded his contract, he was legally obliged to show it.

He couldn't kill. He preferred not to show his contract. Could he take this man out with a sleeping dart?

"Don't even think it, kid." An imp of humour danced in the newcomer's eyes. The stranger drew an actual steel sword. "You're not good enough to get to a weapon faster than I can put this blade through you. Believe me." He held out a hand. "Contract."

A steel sword? There was no way to easily fight anyone using such a weapon. Giving over the contract was Pell's only option. He slid the blowpipe into its sheath on his back and tucked the dagger away. Then he reached slowly into his jacket.

Who was this man? The stranger's hands and forearms were corded and muscular. Fingers calloused from weapons-training. He moved with the unconscious grace of someone who knew his way around a fight. Maybe in his mid-twenties. Long, white-blond hair, tied back. No beard, though, so perhaps from Mamlakah, the jundom to the north.

Ahhh . . .

Pell bowed fractionally, keeping his face in shadow, and held out the square of paper. "All legal, Corin Mal-kin."

"Oh, you do speak? I was beginning to wonder." The glint of humour returned. "And you are a quick one, aren't you?"

Pell said nothing. With luck he might still get out of this. As long as he kept his face hidden. Being identified by a Jun Second's emissary would make finding work in Mamlakah difficult.

A gust of air swept through the open door and the mel-oil lantern flared brightly in the dim-lit room. Pell threw up a hand to shield his face, but too late.

Corin glanced at the body on the floor, then back at Pell. His eyes widened. "Who *are* you?" He bent, reaching for the pulse-point on the body's throat. "This kid looks—"

Pell leapt. He snatched a green-feathered dart from his belt and jabbed toward Corin's thigh. Corin clamped iron-hard onto Pell's wrist and twisted. Pell's fingers were forced open and the dart tinkled to the floor. Folding his elbow, Pell wrenched free. He drove the other elbow into Corin's exposed gut.

With a breathless grunt, Corin skipped backward. He dropped into a fighter's crouch. The steel sword glinted silvery in the dim mel-oil light. Pell pulled out his dagger, horribly conscious of the disparity of weapons. A xiongshou rarely carried a long-bladed weapon. Too hard to conceal.

He flicked two shuriken in quick succession. Corin swayed aside, not taking his eyes off Pell. The throwing-stars clanged off the stone wall and clattered to the floor.

"Do try not to be a complete hmar, kid. I don't want to hurt you," Corin said. "If the contract is legal, we're good." He paused and relaxed his stance, lowering his blade. "Do you know you look like the boy you just killed?"

Pell straightened and threw a quick look at his victim. The young man's face was slack, but the resemblance was undeniable. "I need to get out of Jadid." He sheathed his dagger and handed the contract to Corin.

Corin hesitated and raked both Pell and the body with a shrewd inspection. Then he slid the steel sword back into its scabbard. "Agreed." He unfolded the contract and skimmed it. His brows twitched into a frown. "Signed by Xiaan? No payor listed. Unusual." His frown deepened. "There's something odd going on here."

"You really are the *most* irritating man," a throaty, feminine drawl emerged from the shadows.

Pell tensed, hand on dagger again. He backed up and glanced at the door. Corin spun, keeping both Pell and the newcomer in his line of vision.

Mistress Xiaan emerged into the flickering light. She had shed her golden robe and veil and wore now a plain, dark-yellow house robe. Her grey-streaked hair was pulled tightly back into a bun at the nape of her neck. Her hands were empty and she wore no weapons. Pell relaxed slightly but the burn in his stomach intensified at the sight of her.

"What's going on, Xiaan?" Corin snapped. He brandished the contract. "You signed off on this? Why would you have your Bonded family's heir assassinated?" He pointed at Pell. "And why does this kid look so much like Faktor?"

Pell waited, tightening the grip on his dagger. His heart thudded in his ears. Would she tell the truth?

Xiaan hesitated, her gaze travelling over Pell from head to toe. She smiled faintly, with a hint of old regret. "Because this youngster is Faktor's brother. His twin brother, to be exact."

Pell sucked a sharp breath. He gripped the back of a nearby armchair, his fingertips whitening.

This was about to get complicated.

"What?" Corin let out a sharp breath. "But twins are . . . ah! I see. When Prince Soran's first wife had twin boys you hid one in Weishi House. The common people fear twins because xintou are forbidden to bear them." He smiled wryly. "And most people practically worship the ground you xintou walk on."

"Though clearly you don't," Xiaan said, her reply acid. "But, yes, people are superstitious of twins. Twin boys, especially—because xintou aren't allowed to bear boys, either." She sent Corin an ironic look. When he returned it blandly, she continued, "The princedom of Jadid was in a bad way. We'd had three years of heavy, long winters. So many people were dead and starving that the population was on the verge of revolt against Prince Soran. He and I decided to hide Pell in Weishi House for his own good. To protect him."

"And Soran," Pell noted drily.

"Yes. And your father," Xiaan agreed.

"Well, you hired the right xiongshou." Corin nodded toward Pell. "The kid's efficient, I'll give him that." He touched Faktor's pulse point. He rose again, one hand sliding into his pocket.

The grey dart was gone from the floor.

"Faktor's dead." Corin sent the Xintou a bleak smile. "I'm assuming that was your plan? To kill Faktor and substitute his brother?"

"Dead! But . . ." Xiaan's finely-lined cheeks blanched. She took a step toward the body. "Let me see—"

"Are you accusing me of failing to fulfil my contract?" Pell stepped between her and his brother's body. "That would require a public trial before the Weishi House masters. And an independent observer has declared Faktor dead." He held his breath. Would she try to breach his wards? Dig into his mind? He suppressed a shiver.

She stared first at him then at Corin's bitter smile before heaving a sigh. "What a mess." Xiaan rubbed her face. "No. I won't dispute. You were trained by the best and Master Hao vouched for you." She cast a regretful look at Faktor. One trembling hand covered her mouth and she sank into the faded purple armchair. "It was Faktor's plan. And Yarina's." She covered her eyes. "To hire a xiongshou. Pell, specifically. But he wasn't supposed to kill. Just get Faktor out of the princedom."

"What?" Corin blinked.

Pell waited. There was more, but would she reveal it to this outsider? Would Corin guess?

Xiaan nodded. "You've seen how Prince Soran despises Faktor. Thinks him weak. Faktor tried so hard to be the son Soran wanted,

123

but he could never please him. Yarina is far more fit to rule after Soran. Faktor just wanted out."

"Well," Corin replied sourly, "he's certainly out now. What was your next step? And why get his own brother to murder him. That seems callous . . . even for you." There was a hint of a sneer in Corin's tone and Pell warmed to the northerner.

She stared for a long time at Faktor's still body. Tears shimmered on her lashes.

Pell clenched his jaw, holding back the angry words bubbling behind his lips.

Xiaan glanced at Pell. "We asked for Pell on purpose. I knew that anyone who succeeded in this contract would have to leave Jadid immediately. Faktor is well-liked in certain circles." The lines around her mouth deepened and her throat worked. "We decided Pell should be the one so he would have to leave. Otherwise he would be a potential threat to Yarina's rule if anyone found out he existed."

Pell ground his teeth and swallowed down the urge to fling eighteen years of resentment at the woman. She had deprived him of so much. Not only the lion-head family tattoo, but the family and sense of belonging that accompanied it. Not only a life of privilege and comfort, but the warmth of parents and siblings who cared, rather than the cold backhand of the House Masters or the . . . personal . . . attentions of the senior boys.

"I don't understand," Corin said, frowning. He studied Faktor's face and then Pell's. "They look enough alike. Why *didn't* you just substitute Pell for Faktor?"

"I'm xiongshou," Pell said, quietly. He curled a lip. "Can't have an assassin on the throne of Jadid. Everyone in Weishi House would know me the minute they saw me."

Xiaan opened her thin lips, paused, then nodded without adding anything.

Corin's sharp gaze slid from her to Pell, to Faktor and back to the Xintou. "Lucky for you Prince Soran's second wife birthed Yarina then, huh?"

Twin spots of red coloured Xiaan's pale cheeks. "Indeed."

Pell straightened. "With your permission, I'll withdraw. My contract is complete. I'm no longer welcome in Nanqualea. I'll leave with the next caravan."

Xiaan rose and hurried to him. She reached out a hand toward his cheek but he flinched away, keeping his expression stoic and cool.

Her shoulders slumped and her mouth drooped. "Of course. I'm . . . I'm sorry. More sorry than you can know."

"So am I." Pell turned on his heel and left.

A day later he waited at the caravan departure point on the outskirts of town, the collar of his glass-rabbit-fur jacket turned up, his nose buried deep in a thick wool scarf. He'd used his contract money to buy a sturdy horse, and the gear he would need to camp out in the caravan's train. Then he'd hired himself as a weishi-guard to the caravan master in exchange for passage north across the Jabal Mountains, into Mamlakah.

He glanced back at the ragged rooftops of Nanqualea and ignored a pang of . . . what . . . fear? Regret? It was hard to be sure. There was nothing left for him there.

The great bell of Prince Soran's keep had rung four times, indicating the death of the heir. The day of mourning was over. Faktor's body had been entombed with his ancestors in the crypts beneath the keep. Yarina would be made heir next week. She was popular. The announcement had quelled incipient riots.

Pell twisted his mouth. Yarina was a good choice. Better than he was. The last thing he wanted was to be Bonded telepathically to Mistress Xiaan; the woman who had thrown him away. Now he could start fresh. Maybe go to Madina, capital of Mamlakah. Find work based out of the Weishi House there.

He turned his face from the city and watched the final piles of baggage and timber get loaded onto the brightly-painted caravans. Slowly, the sturdy beasts towing wagons began plodding north, leaving fresh dark trails of muck in the snow-dusted street.

Outside the city's high stone walls, Pell let his shoulders relax. He dragged in a slow breath of sharp, clean air and looked forward to the northern mountain's jagged peaks.

Freedom wasn't far away.

At the sound of near hoofbeats he slewed in his saddle. Two men approached from behind. Both wore thick glass-rabbit-fur jackets, their hoods raised and faces muffled by scarves.

"What took you so long?" Pell asked.

"A minor matter of being dead to overcome," came the reply. The smaller man flung back his thick grey hood.

Pell reached across and gripped the man's forearm in the manner of friends. "Good to see you awake, brother."

Faktor's shy smile widened. "Nice to be awake." He scrubbed a hand over his short-cut dark hair and scratched at the scraggly beginnings of a beard on his pointed chin.

Pell rubbed at his own, smooth jaw. He had chosen not to grow a beard, and his hair would grow back in time. He no longer considered himself of Jadid. He turned to the other rider. "Corin. How did you know?"

The northerner grinned and threw back his hood, his green eyes sparkling in the weak morning sun. He held up a grey-feathered dart.

"Xiongshou normally use black for death. I'd never seen grey—or even heard of it—but it wasn't hard to guess that you were using something to simulate death." He shrugged. "Figured it might be interesting to play along. So?"

"And did you tell Mistress Xiaan or Prince Soran?" Pell fingered his dagger, keeping his face neutral.

"Relax, kid. Yarina's the only one who knows. She came to me after you left. Apparently Xiaan told her Faktor really was dead. Yarina was so upset I had to set her mind at ease." Corin's grin twisted. "And now the future ruler of Jadid owes me. And therefore owes the Jun Second of Mamlakah. Plus, I got a good deal on the next yar-pine shipment because Xiaan was afraid I'd tell someone else the truth."

"Ah." Pell laughed low. "Opportunist."

"Of course! So, do tell—why this big charade?" Corin cocked his head. "Because it wasn't easy swapping the bodies."

127

Faktor chuckled, his dark eyes creasing with ready humour. "You really didn't have to. There's a secret exit out of the crypt. I would have been fine when I woke up. We had it planned."

Corin swiped at his face. A huff of breath emerged as a dense cloud in the cold air. "I think I'm getting old. Why the big magic trick?" He eyed Pell. "That excuse about not being able to be heir because you're xiongshou? Very thin. What's really going on? Why did you want Xiaan to think Faktor was dead?"

Pell looked to Faktor, who shrugged and nodded. "Because she's our mother," Pell said, trying to keep his voice level and leached of bitterness.

Now Corin reared back in his saddle like he'd been slapped. "Twin *boys!* A Bonded Xintou had twin boys? What possessed her?"

Faktor's brow darkened. "Our father's first wife was barren. He wanted a boy. The kin-child laws had just come into effect and Jadid was in turmoil."

Corin sighed, a flicker of old pain shadowing his expression. "So Xiaan decided to produce Soran's heir herself, rather than risk another woman's life."

Pell snorted. "You're giving her too much credit."

"It gets worse," Faktor said. "I found Xiaan's notes about her pregnancy and worked out what she'd done. She's nai-xintou—able to manipulate DNA, but only on her own eggs. By the time Xiaan realised she was having twins, it was too late to abort."

"That still seems like a big risk," Corin said, frowning. "Why not pay a surrogate mother?"

With a bitter laugh, Pell raked the northerner with a wry look. "Imagine how much control she'll have if she was both mother to the heir *and* Bonded Xintou to the Prince? Yarina is hers, too, you know."

"Interesting." A thoughtful frown came over Corin's face. "You could be right. Xiaan needs close watching, I think. But you two aren't . . ." He raised his brows.

"Male xintou?" Pell shrugged. "No. Xiaan made sure of that. We're no danger to anyone."

Corin gave a disbelieving laugh. "So, you're kin-children—illegal. Twins—frowned on. Males born to a Xintou—absolutely forbidden." He slapped Pell on the shoulder. "I don't think you could be more outcast if you tried, kid."

Pell pursed his lips but said nothing. He didn't need sympathy.

"How did you two meet?" Corin asked.

"The last six months of xiongshou training includes studying the layout of the keep," Pell said. "I found Faktor in his hidey-hole. He realised I was the brother Xiaan had hidden away. She never said where she'd hidden me."

"When I found how he'd been raised . . . what they'd done to him there . . ." Faktor shuddered and sent Pell an apologetic look. "I knew I couldn't stay any longer. Neither of us could. So we worked out a plan. He kills me and gets to leave. I die and get to vanish. We both win."

"Pell?" Corin lifted his brows. "What do you get out of this? You have to leave your home." He shivered and pulled his glass-rabbit-fur jacket closer. "Although I do understand the appeal. Anyone who lives in a permanent state of winter is utterly insane."

Pell returned a thin smile. He glanced at Faktor and then at the open road ahead. "I get a brother that cares. Someone who can watch

129

my back." He eyed Corin narrowly. "And I suspect I only stayed alive after the attack on Faktor because you interrupted Xiaan's plans."

"Ahhh . . . interesting. What do you plan to do?" Corin studied him shrewdly

Pell merely smiled, held his intents in silence and gazed north.

With any luck he would also get the opportunity to study Xintou House in Madina.

And a future chance at justice.

About the Author:

Aiki Flinthart has 13 published novels and one non-fiction book, along with numerous short stories published in various anthologies and e-magazines. Her stories have been shortlisted in the Australian Aurealis Awards and she has been twice a top-8 finalist in the USA Writers of the Future competition. When not writing, Aiki likes to practice fantasy-approved hobbies such as martial arts, archery, knife-throwing, lute-playing, and belly-dancing. You can find her on Facebook, Twitter, and Instagram—she's the only Aiki Flinthart—and here:
www.aikiflinthart.com

ETHAN

Talien Jae

"Ethan!" Sophie's voice needled into his ears as Ethan moved down the stairs, sluggish and tired. It was nearly noon, but morning nonetheless for the malcontent.

"What?" He stepped off the landing and turned the corner into the kitchen, reaching for his cigarettes on the bench as soon as he did.

She held out a purple envelope, smiling gently at him. "You've got mail."

Ethan waved it away and moved toward the kitchen door to head outside. "Probably a bill, put it in the bin."

Sophie sighed. "Ethan, it's from the Dioscuri."

Ethan stopped, his hand still on the door handle. "Bin it."

Outside, the air was chilled and fresh, and Ethan clasped his robe as he pulled a cigarette from the deck and lit it.

"Morning." Dana sat at the outside table, a blanket over her legs, a laptop and a still-steaming coffee in front of her.

The door banged shut as Sophie exited the house, purple envelope in hand. "You can't ignore it, they'll know."

"What's going on?" Dana picked up her coffee, wrapped her fingers around it and sat back, looking up from her laptop, forgetting it for a rare moment. She spent her time studying, for the most part. So far she had four bachelor degrees, each one vastly different to the next. Geology, psychology, liberal arts, and anthropology. She liked to keep her mind 'busy'—so she said.

"Ethan's got a letter from the Dioscuri, but he won't even open it."

"Since when do they send snail mail?"

Ethan snorted. "Right?" He sat down opposite Dana. "I'm surprised they sent anything at all, considering one of them is 'busy' all the time and the other one seems to be nothing more than a stoner."

"You can't say that!" Sophie said, looking around nervously.

Ethan shook his head. It wasn't like they were watching, but Sophie was always one for dramatics. "Pollux is high *all* the time."

"It's true, he is," Dana said. Her gaze flicked from Ethan to Sophie, their mouths open. "What? I had to meet with them last week."

"How often do you meet with the Dioscuri?" Sophie asked.

"First time in two centuries."

"Why *you*? You're a Sag, there's no reason for them to want to talk to you," Ethan said, suspicious.

Dana rolled her eyes. "What do you *think* they wanted to talk about?"

"Why their sudden interest in me? I've not done anything, not that I know of."

Sophie held out the envelope again. "Maybe that's the problem? But you won't know until you open it, will you?" She waited a moment before stamping her foot. "Take the damn envelope, Ethan, I want to see what it says!"

ETHAN

Ethan took the envelope. He didn't want to read it, and particularly not in front of anyone else. If the Dioscuri had decided to summon him, then things weren't looking good for his future. If it was a simple assignment, then he should be fine, but assignments usually came through email—had for years. Right now, he didn't want to know either way. They would know he had the envelope now, just as they would know when he opened it. It was who they were. They knew everything. Well, everything to do with their representatives. They would know he hadn't completed any assignments recently. The last decade at least. He'd been busy—and avoiding it, if he were honest with himself. Representatives only dealt with babies due to be born on the cusp of a zodiac. That was their job. Go to the house or hospital, find the mother. If the baby's future showed certain traits, it would be assigned a zodiac, determining their dominant sign. If not, the job went to the opposing sign's representative. Those not born on the cusp were left to the sign they were born under, but cusp babies were complicated, their destinies woven with positive and negative energies. The wrong sign assigned to a cusp baby could spell disaster.

He put out his cigarette in the ashtray. "I need coffee. And food." He stood and tucked the envelope in his dressing-gown pocket.

Dana leant forward, her eyes focusing on her laptop screen again. "Put enough water in for me, will you?"

Ethan nodded and went inside, escaping Sophie's glare. She didn't follow him. He put the kettle on, then went upstairs to his room, closed the door and sat on his bed.

He ripped the envelope open and pulled out the stark white paper inside.

An address and a date and time. Nothing more. *42 Wickenbrook Crescent, 20th of June. 8:54pm.*

"Well, that's not specific at all," he mumbled to himself. Dead-centre of the cusp. Normally, when he was assigned babies, he had at least a month before they were born to deal them their zodiac, not this late in the cycle. It was already the seventeenth, and the cusp was due to begin that night. It was on the outskirts of his zone, too.

Why this baby? After all this time, why send him an assignment? He'd not completed a job in ten years or more; not that it mattered much, there was another Gemini in the area, had been for about six years. They'd not spoken. Geminis didn't blend well. He placed the letter in his pocket but left the envelope on the bed. No doubt Sophie would come looking for it—probably shift into a mouse or something, he thought. She had a problem with boundaries even at the best of times.

Downstairs, the kettle had boiled. Ethan prepared Dana a cup first. Knowing she liked her coffee strong, he poured the instant into the cup rather than use a spoon. He filled it up with hot water and set the kettle aside. He placed some bread in the toaster and retrieved the margarine from the fridge. The vegemite lived on the bench, mostly because Sophie never put it away. He unscrewed the lid in anticipation.

"Morning."

Ethan didn't turn around. "Morning, James." He pulled the letter from his pocket and passed it over. James unfolded it as he reached into the cupboard to pull out two teabags—he always had two, even if the teabag was listed as extra strong. James refolded the letter and passed it back.

"You're going to have to go, you know that, so why fight it?"

134

"They'll send someone else," Ethan said, placing his toast on the cutting board. James, a representative for Aquarius, was probably the truest to his sign than anyone else in the house. Aloof? Check. Progressive? Also check. Lack of emotional expression? Triple check.

"No, they won't. They've chosen you to deal this child their zodiac, which means they'll make sure it's you who does it." He paused, watching Ethan closely. "You remember what happened to the last Scorpio who lived here."

"De-deified, probably." It was rare, but it happened. A representative could be stripped of their immortality, their gifts taken away in an instant. It didn't seem like something the Dioscuri would do, though, even if they were angry.

"Not *probably*. She was left with nothing. No memories. No family."

"She was a bit unbalanced though."

"She was certifiable." James stopped dunking his teabags, and Ethan frowned—there was no water left in the kettle. "Will you go tonight?" James asked.

"No." Ethan left the kitchen, taking his toast with him to the lounge room, not bothering with a plate.

Ethan spent the next two days in his dressing gown, headset on, ignoring the world around him. It was James who came in to draw him from his makeshift nest on the couch.

"You need to get dressed and get moving," James said, absentmindedly watching the TV screen.

135

Ethan pulled his headset down. "I've got time."

"Not if there are delays on the train line."

Ethan groaned. James was right. He was always right. He put his controller on the coffee table, shifting the mix of dirty plates, glasses and mugs to make space for it.

"If you don't go, the Dioscuri won't take it lightly." James looked over at him. "I haven't known them to keep tabs on a rep for decades, and they've had both Dana *and* Soph in already."

Ethan looked up. "Both of them?"

"Both." James sighed gently. "You know you're going to go, so perhaps stop delaying." He turned and left the room without another word.

After showering and dressing, Ethan left the house. He did not own a car, so he had to leave early; trips across town took much longer than they were supposed to, the public transport in the area usually being delayed either by roadworks, rail works, or just *because*. That, and he hadn't caught transport since his last job interview two years ago.

It wasn't that he didn't want a job, he thought, looking at the overhead timetable. Five minutes until the next train. He just couldn't be bothered searching for one. Was there any point? Really? The Dioscuri paid for the house they lived in, along with the other heads, Leo, Sagittarius, and Aquarius. The representatives of each sign usually lived together, though not all in the same house. The houses were nice enough though; no mould, plenty of space, working plumbing. It was free, after all. The food wasn't, though. He'd been happily living off James, much as Dana did. James was a corporate lawyer, so it wasn't like he didn't have the money to burn.

It took three hours to get to his stop, but he still had six streets to traverse before he got to the house. He started walking and his phone rang.

"Ethan, it's Sophie." Her voice was hurried, frantic.

"What's wrong now?" The last time she had called him it was to yell at him for something. Leaving a plate on the table? No, that wasn't it. Ah, hair in the sink. That was it.

"The Dioscuri want to see you."

He stopped in his tracks. "What, now? I'm nearly there!"

"They came here first, thinking you were still at home. I told them you'd gone, but the herald didn't care. Said he had been told to get you and that was what he'd do."

"Hi."

Ethan turned, startled. Beside him stood a tall man dressed in a neat suit.

"Soph, I gotta go."

"But—"

He hung up on her. "I'll be late," he said.

"Not my issue, mate." The man reached out a hand and placed it on Ethan's shoulder. The dizziness came first, as it always did, and Ethan stumbled as they appeared at the Dioscuri's headquarters.

The Twins—the Dioscuri as they had been known for millennia—certainly had a taste for the ostentatious. It had been a long time since Ethan had been here, and last time their headquarters had been in a much smaller house. This was an enormous building, or so he could see from the window. How high up were they? Thirty floors? Forty? Not that it mattered, there was no escape from here. He moved to one of the high-backed leather chairs and sat down, glad to be off his feet.

"Ethan?"

He looked up. A receptionist dressed in a smart pantsuit smiled gently at him.

"They are ready for you."

Hmph. Last time they had kept him waiting for over an hour.

Inside the office, Castor sat behind a desk in an impeccable suit, while Pollux sat on the couch, dressed much the same but without a suit jacket. He was also missing a tie, and his wrinkled shirt was unbuttoned and untucked. Despite his appearance, he looked unusually sober. Ethan said nothing but stood in front of the desk, waiting for Castor to look up.

"Sit."

Ethan moved to the chair and sat down, sitting nervously on the edge.

Castor looked up. "It is good to see you again, Ethan."

"Same," Ethan said.

Pollux laughed. "Bullshit," he said. "You hate being here."

"It's true, you can't lie here, Ethan." Castor rose from his chair and rounded the desk, leaning back to sit on its edge. "We know you don't want to be here."

"Or anywhere," Pollux said.

Castor gave his brother a look, sending him to silence. "Indeed. Now, you have no job, is that right?" he said, looking at the sheet of paper in his hands.

How much had Dana told them? "Er, yeah."

"And you currently undertake no studies."

ETHAN

"I don't."

"What do you do with your time?"

Ethan shifted uncomfortably. "I play games, I guess."

"Good." Castor returned to his chair and sat. "We have a new assignment for you." He tapped at his computer and spun the screen. "This is Mary, she is due to have her baby very soon, and we want you to guide the child."

"Guide the—What about the kid I'm supposed to be assigning?"

"Same child. More information has come to our attention. The Cancer representative has already inspected the child and it will be a Gemini. I still want you to confirm that, though. If the child is to be a Gemini, it will need a strong guiding figure in their life. That figure will be you."

"I haven't been a guide in centuries, and last time . . . well, last time it didn't work out so well."

"No shit. Right screwed that up, didn't ya?" Pollux said, standing. He wandered over to a drinks station and pulled the cork on a bottle of wine. In moments Ethan and Pollux each had a glass in hand. Ethan hated wine.

Castor frowned momentarily. "We're not asking, not this time. We know last time didn't end as desired, but that happens sometimes. Your lack of direction since has been problematic, but lately you've stopped working assignments and we cannot have that. It's important to us that each representative have *something* to busy themselves with, otherwise"—he looked to his brother briefly, who was once again sitting on the couch—"they fall to addiction, or they become listless, much as you have. When that happens, our options are limited."

"De-deification."

Pollux grinned, leaning back into the cushions. "Yup. See? He's not as dense as I thought he was. He gets it."

Ethan's heart thumped in his chest. Surely they wouldn't do that for so small a transgression?

"Relax," Castor said, feeling his tension. "Provided you guide the child all will be fine. It's a long commitment, but you of all representatives are well suited to this particular child."

"How so?"

"You are ruled by curiosity, it's one of the reasons you were originally selected as a Dioscuri representative."

Night had fallen by the time Ethan was returned to his assignment. While he hadn't had to stay long with the Dioscuri, he'd had to wait for a trip back. 42 Wickenbrook Crescent was a small house; the yard was untended, but the house seemed in good order. The lights were on inside. Ethan grumbled to himself. He could shift form, of course, or he could phase. He'd not shifted in a long time—last time he had been a cat and he'd gotten hit by a car. James had picked him up from a bunch of bushes at a nearby park. It hadn't been glamorous.

Ethan phased before he walked into the yard. The sturdy front door was no obstacle. He always loved seeing other people's homes. Some were clean, so clean it was as if no one had ever lived in them. Not this one. It wasn't messy, but it was lived in. He wandered through the rooms unseen. In the lounge room, a man snored on a desk chair in front of his computer. The TV lit the room—

advertisements for the most part. Mary wasn't in here, nor was she in the adjoining kitchen. He eventually found her in the bedroom; half dressed, and half asleep on the queen-size bed. The room was a bit of a mess, but no worse than his own. Clothes had been dumped on the floor, there were baskets of washing in the corner—clean or dirty he couldn't tell—and a damp towel hung on the door.

The alarm clock on the bedside table read 8:52pm. Ethan pulled the note from his pocket. He wouldn't do anything until 8:54pm. The time given by the Dioscuri was the best time to see its zodiac, and this baby was, apparently, difficult. Cancer might have checked the baby early—the zodiac was always given early—but at this stage of the cusp, the baby would be here soon; a day, a day and a half at most. *I have to be certain.*

Mary would go in to labour soon, and already the baby inside pulled at Ethan, demanding its zodiac; demanding that a choice be made. Ethan moved closer. Mary's eyes fluttered briefly before closing, she was exhausted and uncomfortable, and he was once again glad he would never have to bear a child. She rolled to her side, an effort in her state.

8:53pm. Ethan moved forward. It was never easy to touch a person while they were sleeping, it felt a little creepy, but they couldn't feel it as anything more than a slight churning in their bellies. He leant across the bed and gently placed his hands on her side. Immediately the baby kicked his palm and Mary shifted in her sleep. Ethan repositioned.

8:54pm. Ethan closed his eyes and felt his power surge. It had been so long since he'd used it and he relished the feeling of lightness, his negative energy dissipating until there was nothing but a steady calm. The baby squirmed, impatient. Ethan searched for its future, for the traits that would guide him in his decision. *Duality.* Similar to the last child he had acted as a guide for. Except this child was *pure* duality, there was no lean to either side. The last had leant slightly to the side of Cancer, but not enough to be a true Cancer. Everything about this child was Gemini. As true a Gemini as Castor or Pollux; maybe more so, as their duality was split. There was something special about this child, unseen. There was nothing more, just an intensity that Ethan had not felt before. Things could be wonderous for this little human. They would bring immense change, but for good or for bad Ethan couldn't tell. The last child had fallen, fallen to the wrong side. Fallen to a darkness Ethan hadn't been able to pull him out of, and the boy had done much damage to humanity. It was Ethan's biggest failing.

But this child . . . Ethan's curiosity bloomed. This child could go either way. The little girl stood on a razor's edge, neither here nor there, each potential future as beautiful and as terrible as the next. He knew he would stay with her until the end, even just to see where the adventure would take them.

About the Author:

Talien works in the publishing industry and Ethan is her first foray into publishing her own work. She lives in western Victoria with her family, writes whenever she gets the chance, and lives and breathes speculative fiction.

ÐREAMKILLER

Stephen Herczeg

Blood misted his vision. The air was thick with it. The flowers on the walls were crossed with crimson slashes that ran down to the deep-pile carpet, staining it forever red.

He raised the knife and plunged it again and again, spraying scarlet streaks across the wallpaper. Congealing blood hung down like stalactites turning the room into a carnal grotto of death. The light silk sheets on the bed had become a macabre canvas unfit for even a mortician's gurney.

Exhausted, the killer finally stopped and dragged air deep into his lungs. The broad smile plastered across his face perfectly complimented the glazed look in his murderous eyes.

His naked body was painted in his victim's life blood. The thought that he had so intimately shared her last moments filled him with glee.

He raised the knife to his mouth and ran his tongue along the blade, relishing the coppery taste.

Before him lay the devastated remains of his victim. A line of drool gathered at his lips and ran down his chin to drip into that crimson horror.

Her beautiful blonde features were now streaked with red. Her bright blue eyes lay open, a dazed expression staring off into the infinite void that had claimed her soul. His attack had been so quick she never had a chance to blink.

Climbing off the bed, he scanned the room. The bedside clock lay upside down on the floor, it flashed the time as eight o'clock. Darkness poured in through the uncurtained window.

A bright glow in the corner grabbed his attention. He twisted and discovered a laptop computer. A login screen with a strange helix design cast a dull blue glow before it. He walked over and shut the computer, annoyed at the light it threw.

As he returned to the bed, he spied his reflection in the full-length mirror on the back of the bedroom door.

He liked what he saw. Dark hair glistened with sweat and blood on his chest. Blood streaked the well-defined muscles of his chest and stomach. He smiled wide at the defiant enthusiasm of what thrust out proudly beneath his abdomen.

When he saw his face, his expression dropped into one of absolute horror.

Screaming "no, no, no," at his reflection, he strode forward and punched the mirror, shattering his reflection into a million disparate images.

They floated across his dreamscape as another voice invaded his mind.

"Bruce. Bruce," the voice intruded into the dream.

Mary McKinley looked down at her husband Bruce, as he shouted and writhed about his side of the bed. She tried to catch a thrashing arm, but he pulled free of her grip and almost cracked her in the head on the return swing.

"Fuck," she cried, before grabbing for his arms again, "Bruce, it's a dream. Just a dream. Wake up. Bruce, please, you're scaring me" she shouted, her voice trailing off to a whimper and finally sobbing as tears formed and flowed.

Bruce's body succumbed and lay still. His eyelids fluttered and opened, then he sat bolt upright, his body bathed in sweat, hair plastered to his head.

She watched his face turn towards her. His eyebrows creased as he saw her tears.

"It happened again. Didn't it?" he said, his face dropping into a mask of sorrow.

Mary simply nodded through her sobs.

"I'm so sorry," he said, reaching out and dragging Mary into his arms. "I'll go see the doc tomorrow."

"Please. You're scaring me," she sobbed.

They lay down in each other's embrace. Mary felt Bruce's rock-hard presence. She shifted away to avoid any misunderstandings. That was something she didn't need or want right now.

There was only one thought on her mind.

What the Hell is happening to you?

"It was like I was there, but I wasn't there," Bruce said.

Dr. Debra Cox, the police psychiatrist, sat back in her chair and jotted down notes on her lined pad.

"Was that any different to your other dreams?" she asked.

Bruce thought for a moment then shook his head. "No, no it wasn't. I think they've always been that way. I'm just an observer. A voyeur of myself acting out the murders in the same way as the killer."

"Why do you think that is?"

"I have no idea. Why would I dream of being a murderer? Of killing those women? I don't even like reading or watching that sort of thing."

"But you became a policeman? Moved into homicide?"

"Because I want to *stop* people like the Tarot Killer, not because I want to be around them."

"You mentioned the dream stimulated you."

Bruce closed his eyes and sighed. "Yes." His felt flushed, his cheeks reddened at the thought. "I don't know where that came from. As I said, nothing like that would ever turn me on normally. I hate the site of blood. I put up with it 'cause of my work, but if I can avoid it I will."

"We have established that you have deep seated anger issues. That's why you're here after all."

"It only happened once. And I've said it time and time again. It was as if someone else was in control of me. Like the dreams. Exactly like the dreams. Someone else was controlling me. I was just an observer. The same thing happened with Lewis."

Lewis had been a case Bruce worked on at the beginning of his career in homicide. He was a known serial rapist and the body of a woman had turned up in a park near his home.

Bruce and his previous partner were sent to bring Lewis in for questioning. Lewis had tried to escape. Bruce stopped him. For good. Lewis never physically walked again, but he walked away from any charges they could lay on him. Bruce had been suspended for twelve months and forced to see Debra Cox once a fortnight from then on.

"Okay. Now this latest dream. The victim? Was she one of the past victims you've dreamed about, or someone new?" she asked.

"She wasn't any of them. I've never seen her before in my life."

"Maybe you picked up on someone you met or saw in the street and painted a fantasy around her?"

"Why? The thought of what I was doing in that dream disgusts me. I could never treat another human being that way, especially a woman."

"That could be the difference between your ego and your id. Your outer voice and your inner voice. Outwardly, you recoil from any thought of such actions, but inwardly there may be a deep-seated joy from such thoughts."

Bruce looked at her with disgust. "There can be no joy in killing."

"Fair enough, maybe not joy. Maybe it's more a case of those thoughts driving your unconscious mind. You painted an entire scene in your mind just from the facts related to this case. You used a victim that you imagined. It may be you're getting too close to this case. Too close to this man, this Tarot Killer. It's affecting your mind and soon it will affect your life."

"Then I need to catch this killer and close the case."

"Or?"

"There is no or. I need to close this case. If not just to stop the killer but to save face with my superiors."

"And there we may have the driving force itself. You're so worried about failure that you may be causing your mind to create its own narrative."

Bruce looked at her blankly as he tried to reconcile what she was saying.

Debra stared at him, waiting for a response. When he remained quiet, she continued.

"Or you may have subconsciously been assessing all the facts and constructed a cohesive narrative that will lead to a resolution to your case."

Bruce's eyes widened. He stared into space for a moment then his eyes returned to Debra's face. "You've hit the nail on the head." He rose from the couch and headed for the door.

"Bruce, where are you going? We haven't finished."

He stopped and turned back to her. "I need to get back to my desk. What you said makes perfect sense. I must have put all the facts together and worked out the next victim." He looked away and waved his hands around to punctuate his points, continuing to speak more to himself than to his psychiatrist. "All I've got to do is work out how I came up with the victim. I know what she looks like. I sort of know the type of house she lives in. I may even know where she works."

He turned and left before Debra could say another word.

Bruce stared at the evidence board. The words "Tarot Killer" were written across the top. Four Queen cards from a standard tarot deck were pinned just below the title. Of the four cards, the Queens of Cups, Swords and Wands had photographs of pretty young women pinned beneath them. Handwritten notes about each woman were scrawled in a column below their photographs.

The space beneath the Queen of Pentacles was devoid of a photograph. Scrawled below it were individual words such as "practical", "capable", "organised", "fit", "healthy", and "athletic". A couple of lines had been added later with "Businesswoman?" "Lavish lifestyle?" included.

A large map of Canberra was pinned next to the evidence board. Coloured string lines reached from each of the victim photographs to places on the map. Red for their discovered location, yellow for their place of work.

Bruce reread the Queen of Pentacles' description and mumbled to himself. "Practical, capable, fit." He moved to the map and focused on the three pins denoting the victim's workplaces. All were on Bunda Street, within two blocks of each other.

Interesting, but there could be thousands of workers in that area.

The yellow pinned buildings were nestled amongst several others with prominent names below them. Bruce tapped them with his pen.

Fit. Capable. Organised. Maybe a gym close by? Maybe in the building itself? Who's got time to travel to a gym?

"Hey, Cooper," Bruce yelled as he peered over his shoulder.

149

Constable Daphne Cooper, recently assigned to help Bruce, looked up with a start. A touch of guilt on her face.

"Sir?"

"Can you do a search of gymnasiums or fitness centres around Bunda Street, between Akuna and Mort, and up to Cooyong Street, please."

"Yes Sir." Her attention went back to her computer and she frantically typed and clicked away.

Bruce glanced down at the writing pad in his hand. He'd scrawled the design from his dream, a strange helix pattern. Cooper walked over to Bruce and handed him the list of gymnasiums he had requested.

He thanked her and scanned the list. As she moved away, he asked, "Can you give me a list of companies in those buildings and, if possible, links to their websites?"

"Sure," she said.

"I assume you thought homicide would be all gun fights and car chases, not trawling through piles of useless information?" he said

A slight smile crossed her lips. "No problems there," she said, "It beats traffic duty and if it tracks down that asshole, all the better." She blushed slightly when she realised she'd sworn.

Bruce chuckled. "I like your enthusiasm."

Cooper returned to her computer and began the search.

Bruce's train of thought was broken by his partner, Kevin Dubrough, walking into the office. Kevin shucked off his coat and hung it on the coat rack. "What's this?" he asked, approaching Bruce.

"I've added the victims' workplaces. All of them worked in an area of four city blocks."

150

"So does about half the city," said Kevin.

"True, but if our guy is sticking to the Tarot cards, then the next Queen will be a businesswoman, which means he'll stick to the same hunting ground." Bruce checked his list and put green pins in the buildings that had fitness centres. "These are buildings with gyms."

Kevin looked Bruce up and down. "Why don't you just use the gym here?"

Bruce gave him a withering look. "Work with me here, smart arse. If the killer is hunting a career woman who keeps fit, then she will probably use a gym near her employer. Saves time."

"Okay," replied Kevin.

Cooper brought several pages over and handed them to Bruce with a shy smile. As Kevin said hello to her, the smile dropped, and she scurried back to her desk.

"You're married," said Bruce.

"So are you. What's this?"

"The businesses in those buildings. I reckon we're looking for a highflyer, a lawyer, an accountant, maybe even as high as a CEO."

"And young and attractive?" said Kevin.

Bruce looked up, slightly confused, "Yeah? Why?"

Kevin smiled. "Good luck with that in this town."

Bruce stood in front of the towering edifice of glass and steel. His city wasn't huge, but it was growing. Buildings like the one before him were evidence of that.

A swarm of people moved in and out of the front doors. He focused on them for a moment, trying to detect the face of the female victim he'd seen in his dream. His detective's brain overrode his hope and pushed him forward into the crowd.

An hour before he had argued with his partner over his theories. Kevin had been useless, preferring to poke fun at Bruce's ideas rather than contribute anything useful. To Bruce's relief, the Captain had stepped into the room and told Kevin he was needed to advise on another case for the rest of the afternoon.

That freed up Bruce to focus his attention on tracking down the mystery woman, if she even existed.

Cooper's list had been gold. She had sent Bruce the electronic copy as well.

Bruce had worked his way down the list of companies until, magically, the company logo from his dream materialised on screen. "Obstrago," he'd declared, disturbing Cooper who had looked up and questioned him. He'd shrugged her off, apologising for his outburst.

Obstrago was a financial management company located on the fifth, sixth and seventh floors of the Baxter Building on Bunda Street.

Clicking on the personnel link on their website, he had faced a cavalcade of middle-aged white male faces. Every single executive position was taken by men.

Damn, Kevin was right.

He resigned himself to reverting to old school detecting. On his feet. Which had brought him to the front courtyard of the Baxter building.

The lift doors opened up onto a lavish entry foyer. A pretty young receptionist sat behind a large wooden desk. She glanced up at Bruce and smiled, then continued a phone conversation over her headset.

Bruce noticed a series of photos along one wall. There were more photos than just the six he'd seen on the website. He strode over and scanned them.

Luckily, they weren't just a standard rogue's gallery of past and present executives, they were the photos of the current executives and upper management.

Within moments, Bruce's gaze fell on the bright blue eyes and blonde hair of the woman from his dream. She was Helen Smith, the Head of Marketing for Obstrago and Blazard, their sister company.

He was transfixed and growing even more confused. All the evidence pointed to his dream being real. First the strange design that led him to Obstrago, now the photograph of the woman from his dream.

Pictures flashed across his mind of the dream. The blood spraying. The knife, rising, falling. The stench assaulted his nose. The sound of the knife plunging into meat rang in his ears. He was both repulsed and excited all at once. He felt a familiar swelling in his pants and cursed himself under his breath.

A voice snapped him out of his confusion.

"Can I help you?"

He turned and found the young receptionist staring up at him. A look of concern crossed her face as she saw the strange expression on Bruce's face.

He quickly recovered himself and strode across to the reception desk. He dragged his wallet out of his pocket and flashed his identification. "Hi, sorry to bother you, I'm Detective Bruce McKinley with the metro police. I'm working on a case and one of your employees," he fished out his small notepad and flipped it open to a page of unintelligible scrawls and read for a moment, "sorry, a Miss Helen Smith was named as a witness. I needed to follow up on a few questions. I know she's a work horse so thought I'd catch her here," he finished, lying through his teeth.

The receptionist turned away for a moment and tapped a few keys on her computer. She looked slightly shocked at the result. "That's strange," she said, "Miss Smith hasn't been in all day." She looked up at Bruce. "I don't think she's missed a day of work since I joined the company. I can try her mobile if you like?"

"That's not needed. Do you have a home address? I might be able to check up on her in case she's ill and can't come to the phone."

"Sure." She glanced back at the screen. "It's 221 Empire Circuit, Forrest."

Bruce scrawled it down, smiled at the girl and said thank you before turning to leave.

"Say hi for me," she said.

"Not a worry," said Bruce over his shoulder, but worry was all he had on his mind. Too many things were coming true. Too many things he should never have known.

Kevin knocked on the driver's side window.

Bruce slid the window down and acknowledged his partner.

"Made good time, traffic's light at this time of night," Kevin said. He looked across the street at Helen Smith's house. He shivered and pulled his coat tighter. Even in the dull glow from the streetlights, he could tell it was a pretty expensive place. "Well, she's got good taste in houses anyway," Kevin said. "Seen anything?"

Bruce nodded at the car in the driveway and the three cars parked on the street. "The Porsche is hers. Those other three are owned by the kids of her neighbours."

Kevin looked at the cars, then pointed to a dark van further down the street. "What about the van?"

Bruce peered at the screen on his phone. "Stolen. About two days ago. Could have been abandoned but that seems a little too convenient."

"Any movement inside?" Kevin asked.

They both looked at the house. There were lights on in the lower and upper floors.

"I reckon that's her bedroom upstairs," Bruce said. "I've been watching for a while. It's been quiet, no movement."

"What do you want to do?"

"I've called it in, just in case. So, the question is, do we wait or go in now?"

"Your case, your call," Kevin said.

Bruce smiled. "In that case, I say we go in."

They walked across the street together, pausing at the path that lead to the front door. They stared at the windows, searching for any shadows, any movement that would indicate someone was inside other than Helen Smith.

Kevin checked his watch. "It's almost eight o'clock. Even if she's been sick, you'd expect some noise or a TV flicker or something."

"Yeah. That's what I reckon. I'll ring the bell," said Bruce as he started to move towards the door.

Kevin held up his hand. "Hang on." He pointed at the first-floor window.

A shadow moved across the curtains. Its arm rose, something long and thin in its hand, then it fell. A line of dark sprayed across the curtain.

"Oh God," gasped Bruce, his eyes wide in terror.

"Holy crap," shouted Kevin.

Bruce sprinted for the front door, kicked it once and burst through.

Bruce barrelled into the bedroom and froze. The scene before him was exactly like his dream, except for the man straddling the dead woman on the bed. He was overweight, bald and very ugly.

The killer cocked his head at Bruce and leered. A line of drool hung from his mouth.

For a brief moment, Bruce's eyes fell to the victim. His detective's mind took everything in. The blonde hair, the blue eyes, open and lifeless. The killer. The blood. It was everywhere. All over the bed, the walls, the curtains and ceiling.

The killer stared back. A smile on his face. His body unmoving.

Kevin's shout of "What the fuck?" snapped Bruce from his torpor. He stumbled forward as Kevin shoved him out of the way and rushed towards the murderer.

The killer was quick. He lunged at Kevin, driving the knife deep into his abdomen. Kevin cried out. He struggled with the killer, before staggering backwards, tripping and crashing to the carpet. He let out an anguished scream, his hands wrapped around the handle of the deadly knife protruding from his stomach. Blood poured from the wound and stained his white shirt crimson as he lay panting.

Clouds of confusion broiled in Bruce's head, and crowded in blocking out his view and sending his mind into the darkness of the void.

A command cut through the gloom and brought Bruce back to awareness.

"Detective stop!" said a silhouette in the doorway.

Bruce realised a uniformed constable stood in the doorway, his firearm drawn and aimed at Bruce's head. Bruce's expression dropped into confusion and terror. He looked around. He found himself on the floor, straddling the unconscious blood-soaked mess that was now the killer. Kevin lay against the wall covered in blood. He didn't know where he was. He didn't know how he'd got there. The last thing he remembered was stepping into the room and seeing the killer, nothing else, until now.

"What happened?" he asked, the question directed more at himself than at the constable.

"That's something we'll have to work out downtown," the policeman said.

Bruce sat on the cold hard chair. His hands throbbed, gaining no relief from the surface of the cold steel table they rested upon. He stared down at his split and bruised knuckles. The constables had brought him straight to the station before he could be seen by the paramedics. They were acting on orders from above.

"You should have just shot him." The young uniformed police officer who had been given babysitting duties was looking him up and down. He had the cocksure look on his face that came with youth, a uniform and a badge. Bruce remembered that he'd been a bit like that when he'd started on the force.

"Less paperwork and it would have been finished," he continued. "Now the bastard's gonna get off 'cause of you."

Bruce started to reply when the door sprung open and Captain Peter Nash walked in.

"Collins, out," he said.

The young officer scurried away.

Nash dragged a chair opposite where Bruce sat, scraping the legs across the concrete floor deliberately. He dropped a manila folder full of papers and reports onto the table, then flopped his bulk onto the uncomfortable seat.

He sat forward, resting his chin on his steepled fingers and stared across at Bruce. "What the fuck were you thinking, McKinley?"

Bruce only managed to gape open mouthed before Nash continued.

"That fucker you messed up will probably walk free." Nash paused for a moment to let that sink in. "Yeah, all that work you and Dubrough did on this case. Wasted. A psychopath will walk out of here with a clear record and four bodies on his rap sheet. Just 'cause you couldn't hold in your anger."

"I don't. . ."

"Don't, 'don't' me boy. You've got issues. You've had them for years. This should have been your redemption, but you had to go and fuck it all up. I understand that your partner was wounded. I understand that the scene was horrific." He slapped his chest with both hands. "I would have puked if I'd been there and I've seen sick shit that would curl your nose hairs." He pointed at Bruce. "But, no, you. . . *you* had to go one step over the line. You beat that fuck into a pulp. I'm probably wrong. He may never walk again. Hell, he may never even eat solid foods again. He may never know his name or his face ever again. To be totally honest, it would be best if he just up and died. Easier for me as well. You'll go down for murder and I can wash my fucking hands of you."

Bruce blurted out, "I don't remember any of it. All I remember is stepping into the room. Then it all went black and the next thing I see is a gun pointed at my head."

Nash sat back and stared at Bruce for an uncomfortably long time. Finally, he reached for the file and flipped it open to a page with a sticky note attached to it. He read the report then slid it around for Bruce to see. "That's what you said when you beat up Lewis."

He paused for a moment to let Bruce respond. When there was nothing he continued. "You said you weren't there. It was all dark. Someone else was in control."

Bruce nodded.

"You know what I think?"

Bruce shook his head silently.

"Bullshit. All bullshit. That crap may work with a shrink, but I've been a cop for thirty years. I've seen assholes like you who get off on the violence, of being some sort of self-serving vigilante with a badge. A power freak. I won't have it on my force." He grabbed the file and snapped it shut, making Bruce jump. "If I had my way, you'd be gone. Charged, prosecuted, imprisoned, but there are dickheads above me that want the process followed. Cox will be down here soon to assess you. What happens next is up to her. She'll decide whether you're insane or fit to be prosecuted. Either way you will never be a cop again, not if I have anything to do with it."

Snatching up the file and standing, Nash stormed across to the door and hammered a fist against it.

The uniformed policeman unlocked, opened it and looked in at a shell-shocked Bruce. As Nash pushed past, the constable smiled, a grim smile directed at Bruce. He then shut the door, leaving Bruce all alone with his thoughts.

After twenty minutes of staring at the blank two-way mirror in the interview room, Bruce's thoughts were broken by the door opening and Debra Cox walking in. The grim look on her face told Bruce more than anything else.

She picked up the chair, cast aside by Nash, and placed her pad and pencil on the table. She sat down and looked at Bruce's downcast face for a few moments before speaking. "Do you want to go through what happened?"

Bruce looked up. He was tired and strung out, still nursing swollen knuckles and covered in spots of the killer's blood.

Debra grimaced when she saw his face.

"I've got nothing," he said, "One moment I stepped into that bedroom and saw him straddling her corpse, the next I've got a gun pointed at my head and he's lying beneath me in a pool of his own blood." He held up his bloodied hands. "And I only used these." He dropped his swollen hands back to the table, followed by his head.

"The trouble is you've got history. After all, that's why we meet each fortnight. My original diagnosis was that you are borderline schizophrenic, but after this episode I don't think that's the case."

Bruce looked up into her eyes, his face was alive with pleading.

Her gaze was stoic to the point of indifference. "Can you give me more than 'I don't remember anything'?" She made air quotes with her fingers. "Otherwise I'll have no choice."

Bruce shook his head and dropped his gaze again.

Debra sighed then opened the file and signed the topmost sheet. She closed the file and stood. "That was your official discharge papers. You will be placed on a permanent suspension until your disciplinary hearing is heard. You will undergo psychiatric evaluation, but not by me. They'll release you into your wife's care for now."

She stepped up to the door and turned back. "I'm sorry it's come to this Bruce. I thought we were making real progress, but there's a duality in you that I can't crack, and I just don't understand. We may not see each other again, unless I'm called to testify. I wish you luck. I think you're going to need it." She glanced at his swollen hands. The knuckles were split and still speckled with dried blood. "I'll get someone to fix those for you, then you're on your own." She thought for a moment, then shook her head. "I wish there was something I could do for you Bruce, I really do, but this . . ." She tried to find the words. "This is another level all together."

Mary was quiet and sullen all the way home. Bruce tried to explain but his continuous denial of any fault pushed her further away from him and turned her mood into one of near anger.

After he'd managed to have a shower while wearing plastic bags over his bandaged knuckles, he walked into the bedroom to find an overnight bag sitting on the bed. He turned towards Mary with a shocked look on his face. "Is that for me?"

"No. I'm going over to Sarah's to help her with the kids and keep her company. With Kevin in the hospital, she's one step away from completely losing it. I figured she needed more help than you do," she said, her stern look never wavering.

Bruce's own anger began to rise. He kept it in check, but Mary could see it in his eyes.

"No need to get angry with me," she said, "I'm not the one who lost control and pummelled some guy to mush."

162

"Look, what can I do or say to make you believe me? I blacked out. I don't remember doing any of it. It was as if I wasn't even there," he said.

"Yeah, and I've heard that before," she replied, reaching around him for her bag. "I'll have my mobile if you really need me." She turned back from the doorway. "I mean *really* need me." Her tone suggested he wouldn't and shouldn't need her for at least a couple of days.

Bruce's eyes narrowed. He held back a string of curses and simply said, "Fine. See you when you get back. Give Sarah my best. I'll drop by the hospital when I can."

Mary turned and stormed off, shouting, "Don't beat up anybody on the way," over her shoulder as she left.

Bruce looked at the empty door for a moment, his anger fading to defeat. He flopped backwards onto the bed and heard the door slam shut, followed moments later by Mary's car starting and driving off.

He sat up with his head in his hands and the tears began to flow. "What the fuck is happening to me?"

Bruce found himself sitting on the couch watching the television. He tried to search his memory to work out when he'd left the bedroom and come into the lounge.

Another blackout. My brain is stuffed along with my life.

A horror movie was playing. A young scantily clad woman was moving through a dark house at night. Suddenly, a tall man wearing a mask stepped out before her. He slashed down with a machete and cut her arm off. She screamed in a higher pitch than the human voice box can manage as her stump pumped copious amounts of blood everywhere. The killer stepped forward and severed her head. Her body dropped. The camera moved in on the stump of the bloody neck while the last of her life blood pulsed out across the floor.

Bruce was horrified.

What the fuck is this shit?

He snatched up the remote and changed channels until a boring, but sedate looking panel show appeared. He dropped the remote, laid back and closed his eyes.

Moments later he found himself staring at the television again. The same horror movie was playing. Another young woman was being stalked by the masked killer. She moved down a corridor and ended up in a dead-end room. She turned to see the killer step in behind her. There was nowhere to go. The killer closed in and raised his machete. She screamed.

Bruce threw a hand up to hide the image. He grabbed for the remote and turned the television off.

How the fuck is this happening? I need to get this stupid TV fixed.

He stood up. A blinding wave of pain lashed across his head. He brought the heel of his right hand up to his head and steadied himself with his left.

Christ.

Bruce staggered into the bathroom and headed for the medicine cabinet. He pulled out a pack of headache tablets and popped two out. Cupping his hand, he ran some water in the sink and filled it. He managed to swallow the two tablets and stood with his hands resting on the basin and his head hanging down.

Bruce stiffened and cried out as pain lanced through him. He grabbed at his stomach as his whole body began to tremble. A tearing sensation ran through his stomach. He tore at his shirt, stripping it off to check himself.

Nothing. He could see nothing wrong.

Pain struck again. Bile rose up his throat, gagged in his mouth. He quickly moved to the toilet and fumbled with the seat. Before he could raise it, he fell to his knees and vomited the contents of his stomach, missing the toilet bowl and spraying the wall behind and the cupboard next to it.

Bruce fell backwards and lay on his back gasping for air. His stomach was still churning, pain radiated out and raced down his arms and legs like bolts of lightning. He groaned again, grabbing at his stomach until the pain began to dissipate. Finally, his arms flopped to the floor and he lay back, panting hard to regain his breath.

Then the pain returned. His belly was on fire. He grabbed at it again. And he felt . . . *something*. He tore his hands away and peered down at his abdomen.

What he was seeing was terrifyingly impossible. The skin was stretched as if something pushed outwards. He thrust his hands against the bulging flesh and tried to shove it back inside him, but the momentum within was greater than without.

The bulge grew and flung his hands aside. It stretched outward and formed five protuberances that extended into digits.

It was a hand. Bruce cried out in fear.

The hand pushed outwards and became an arm. The arm thrust out, hinging at an elbow. It grabbed Bruce's jaw and pushed him back towards the floor. Another hand punched out from his midriff and joined the other, grabbing at his face and pushing his head and body down.

A large rounded swelling grew out of Bruce's chest and wrenched itself free. The features began to coalesce into the most recognisable object in Bruce's life. His own face. It smiled; a sickly evil grin directed at him.

This can't be real. I'm dreaming. Got to be.

He willed himself to wake up, but the terrifying vision continued.

The head was followed by a neck and chest, which grew and pushed out of Bruce. He felt like his insides were being torn asunder as the doppelganger swelled and extracted itself from him.

Even with his head held to the ground, Bruce could see that his twin was pleased with the whole experience.

Legs emerged together and finally the nightmarish lookalike stepped out of Bruce's body and stood on its own two feet.

It held up its hands and peered along them, relishing the majesty of its existence. It opened and closed its fists and wiggled its fingers, then looked down at Bruce and smiled widely.

"Do you know how long I've waited for this?" it said in Bruce's voice.

Bruce coughed then replied, "What are you?"

"I'm you. Just not the simple, pathetic excuse for a man you are. I'm the better you. I'm the you with all weaknesses removed."

"Why?"

"I'm sick of being holed up in your stupid mind while you piss away your life. There is so much you could accomplish if you weren't such a weak, waste of manhood."

Before Bruce could think up another question, his twin stepped towards him, raised a balled fist and punched him in the jaw, sending him into oblivion.

The doppelganger felt the pain in its hand and flexed it a few times, smiling widely at the sensation. "Oh, that feels so good." It inspected itself in the mirror, admiring every part of its being before tearing its gaze away and looking through the doorway towards the outside world. "After so long it's time to finally have some real fun."

He sat in Bruce's car and flipped through the contacts in Bruce's phone. He found the one he was after and smiled widely.

That's the one.

He punched the address into the GPS, tapped the garage controller and raised the door. Within a few moments he was headed for his target.

The first act of his new life was to choose a name. Whilst he had dwelt inside Bruce's mind, one name had come up while Bruce investigated the Tarot Killer.

Tyr. The Norse God of War. It seemed a fitting name, all he wanted to do was to destroy, to kill, to wage war on the world that he had only known through the eyes of his detested twin. He would tell his victims to call him Tyr, and then he would relieve them of their pitiful lives.

Those that knew him would think Bruce was having a psychotic episode, especially while he wore Bruce's clothes, but Tyr figured he could still have some fun.

After a quarter of an hour, the GPS told him he had arrived. A modestly unpretentious single-story house with a light burning in one room.

Tyr drove on for a few moments before parking in a dark part of the street. He exited, made his way back to the house and sidled up to the lit window being careful where he stepped to keep any noise down.

Through a break in the curtains he found the object of his immediate attention. They sat up in bed, reading a thick novel. Within moments, they let out a large yawn, stretched and put the novel to one side. The light dropped out as Tyr's quarry settled in for the night.

He grinned widely in the dark and crept away.

Oh, we're gonna have some fun tonight.

He made a quick trip back to the car, grabbing a few items he'd found scattered around Bruce's garage, then went around to the back of the house.

As he'd seen from Bruce's perspective over the years, security in the suburbs wasn't a high priority. The rear door quickly succumbed to Tyr's insistence and he stepped into the darkened kitchen.

A quick search rewarded him with several more items that were to be the main props in this evening's performance and made his way to the bedroom.

The occupant was slumbering quietly, much to Tyr's joy. A quick assessment of her bed almost drew chuckles of delight. The owner of the house had installed a large four-poster bed, which would prove perfect for what he had in mind.

He swiftly and carefully eased feet and hands from beneath the covers and secured each via rope and zip-ties to the four corners of the bed, until the dozing occupant was spreadeagled across the mattress with only the doona to protect her.

Tyr placed his latest acquisitions strategically on the tallboy at the foot of the bed. He then removed all his clothes and folded them neatly, placing them on a nearby chair.

Can't be too careful, don't want to get these messy. Well, not yet anyway.

Satisfied, he moved across to the light switch and vanquished the darkness from the room.

Dr. Debra Cox's eyes scrunched shut in annoyance as the light blasted them. She tried to bring her right hand up to shield her eyes but found it wouldn't move more than a couple of inches. She opened her eyelids and cast a bleary gaze at her hand.

The fog of sleep wouldn't allow her to determine what stopped it. "Was goin' on?" she said in a slurred post-sleep tone.

"Lots of things are going on," said a voice, "Or they soon will be."

Debra stared towards the end of the bed. Her vision finally came into focus and she saw Detective Bruce McKinley standing at the foot of her bed, wearing only an inane grin on his face. "Bruce?" she said. "What the hell are you doing here?"

She pulled her hand towards her, only to find it wouldn't move again. She peered at it and finally realised it was bound to the bedpost. Horror smashed into her brain. She turned back towards Bruce.

Full realisation hit hard.

He's lost it. The other personality has broken through and taken control.

"Bruce?" she said. "Let me go. You don't want to do this."

Tyr stepped forward; a wicked smile crossed his lips. "Oh, but I do." he said. He looked down at his nakedness and realised he was a little overcome with excitement. He chuckled. "I apologise for this. I'm not going to do anything like that to you, honest. You're really not my type. I just didn't want to mess up Bruce's clothes."

"Bruce's clothes?"

"Yes," Tyr said, smiling wider. "Oh, you think I'm Bruce." He laughed out loud. "Excellent. Excellent. I'm not Bruce. I could never be Bruce." His face became a sneer. "That stupid boy scout. I've hated him from the moment I became. I've had to live in that skull of his for years. Always buried down deep. Only on rare occasions could I assert my will and take over."

He stared down at Debra, his smile returning. "But you knew that. You knew all along I was in there. Waiting. You tried to force me deeper. You tried to help him gain control. Those drugs. The hypnotherapy sessions. The counselling. Control. Control. Control. That's all you wanted to do was control me."

He turned around and picked up a large chef's knife.

"Well guess what? I'm free. I'm a new me. And I'm the only one who controls me. Not Bruce. Not you. Not even Mary."

He moved forward; the knife held out before him.

Screams pierced the still night, before falling silent again.

Lights lit up in several houses. Faces appeared at windows. Their shocked owners searched the dimly lit street for a moment before returning to their slumber and the darkness.

Bruce's eyes flicked open. All he saw was a stark white blur. Blinking several times to bring the world back into focus, he found he was still lying on the bathroom floor. He tried to sit up, but his stomach muscles felt dead, like he'd executed several hundred crunches. Tensing himself, Bruce rolled onto his side and managed to push himself into a sitting position.

The smell of vomit stung his nostrils, making Bruce look towards the puddle around the toilet. He made a mental note to clean it up later but crawled from the bathroom until he found the bed and managed to drag himself to his feet.

Seeing the bed, Bruce thought about climbing in and crashing back to sleep. His head ached. His chest and stomach burned. His innards felt like they'd been flushed out with dysentery.

Flashes of memory lashed his brain.

The vomiting, the pain, then the figure. His doppelganger.

No. It was just a dream. It can't be real.

Bruce felt his jaw. His light touch hurt, then he recalled his twin punching him.

Must have hit it on the floor when I passed out.

Putting a hand to his throbbing head, he staggered out into the lounge room. The TV was still droning on with two bubbly breakfast

TV presenters spouting drivel about the latest Hollywood starlet and her new beau.

Bruce's eyes strayed to the TV for a moment, taken in by the bright colours. Dragging them away, he spied the answering machine on the side table. The message light was flashing and displaying four missed calls and messages.

Bruce snatched up the handset and pressed play. Mary's voice came on

"Bruce. I've left a message on your mobile, so am trying the home phone. You need to call me."

He pressed next.

"Bruce. Call me. Something's happened to Kevin." Mary's voice sounded full of tears.

"Bruce. Kevin's gone. I need to talk to you."

The final message had Mary sobbing uncontrollably and barely able to control herself. "Bruce. They say it was you. I need to talk to you now."

Another voice, Sarah's, came over the phone. Bruce couldn't understand it but heard Mary's next sentence. She still sobbed through each word. "What? He's here? Okay."

The message cut off.

Bruce quickly dialled Mary's number. The phone went straight to voicemail. "Damn," he said. "Mary, it's Bruce. I'm coming now."

He hung up then saw Kevin's face on the TV. Bruce grabbed the remote and turned up the volume.

"Detective Kevin Dubrough was injured during the arrest of the man known as the Tarot Killer and has been recovering in Central

Hospital. This morning Detective Dubrough was found dead in his room. The victim of multiple stab wounds."

"Holy crap!"

"Witnesses claim to have seen a man enter Detective Dubrough's room early this morning. The description we have of that man seem to indicate it may have been Detective Dubrough's partner, Detective Bruce McKinley."

The screen changed showing Bruce's picture.

"Detective McKinley has been on suspension after he assaulted, Henry Parlow, the man arrested for the Tarot killings, who is also recovering not far from Detective Dubrough's room."

A reporter's face came on. "We now go to a live press conference with Police Captain Peter Nash." The screen changed to show Nash.

Nash looked down the camera and straight at Bruce. "Our investigations are unclear as to the identity of Detective Dubrough's killer, but we are investigating all avenues at this stage."

A reporter piped up with a question. "Is Detective McKinley a suspect?"

"At this stage, all relevant suspects will be questioned, Detective McKinley is high on that list and will be interviewed in due course."

Bruce turned the TV off and stood staring at the blank screen for a moment.

He's real. It wasn't just a dream.

Flopping onto the couch, Bruce dropped the remote next to him. His mind reeled.

How? How can he be real? How can this be happening?

He dropped his head into his hands.

That's impossible. It's got to be someone else. Someone that looks like me.

His head shot up from his hands.

Yeah. They look like me, that's all.

Realisation hit.

Mary. If he killed Kevin, he might try to find Mary.

Bruce looked frantically around the room.

Where the hell is my phone?

Bruce searched the room, becoming even more frustrated as he realised his phone was missing. On the phone table, the bowl where they kept their keys was empty.

Fuck! He's got my keys and my phone.

A distant police siren cut through the early morning silence, drawing Bruce's gaze towards it.

Shit! I need to get to Mary. If they're here for me, I'll never get away.

Bruce grabbed the spare key hanging from the connecting door to the garage and ducked through to find that both cars were gone.

"Bastard."

Bruce headed straight for the steel locker beneath his work bench. He spun the combination wheels and the lock opened with an audible click. Reaching in he pulled out a small package wrapped in a greasy loose-weave cloth.

The gun was a small Smith & Wesson Model 10 with a four-inch barrel. Bruce had bought it a few years back off another officer who'd obtained several when they were decommissioned over a decade ago. Bruce only wanted it for a bit of fun down at the police range. He liked the feel as it was different to his own police issue Glock 22 automatic. Sometimes Mary came to the range too. She was almost better than him.

Grabbing some bullets from a box of ammunition, he loaded the cylinder before snapping it back into place and making sure the safety was on. Bruce put a few extra bullets into his pocket and tucked the gun into the waistband of his jeans. The cold steel against his skin sent a shiver up his spine.

When he heard the police cars pull up outside, Bruce moved towards the back door of the house.

Crap.

After unlocking the back door, he hurried through and made it to the rear fence when he heard his front door burst open.

Christ. They're not kidding around.

Bruce grabbed the top of the fence and pulled himself over. He'd only met Andrew, his rear neighbour, a couple of times, but always admired how neat and tidy his yard was. Now, Bruce just hoped he wasn't home.

Creeping past the side of the house, he found his way to the side gate and peered through the slats. The street beyond was quiet. It was a workday, so most of the neighbours would have left by now. Unlatching the gate, he quietly moved through.

The street was quiet, with only a couple of cars parked along it.

Need a car.

There were three parked on the street. Two were modern. Very hard to break into. The last one was about twenty years old. Bruce smiled and moved patiently, but with purpose, to the passenger's side.

Bruce checked the door and found it unlocked. Part of him was elated, the copper in him couldn't stop thinking about how stupid people could be. Bruce opened the door and crawled across to the driver's seat. The ignition was empty, so too the console, even the last spot that people hide keys, the driver's visor, was empty.

At least they had some sense.

Reaching beneath the ignition keyhole, Bruce pulled out a bunch of wires, recalling his short course on vehicle theft. After stripping the plastic coating with his teeth, he tapped the wires together. The car sparked to life. He gently gripped the steering wheel and pulled away from the curb.

Great, now they can add car theft to my growing list of offences.

After twenty minutes of navigating mid-morning traffic and scanning each window and mirror for flashing blue and red lights, he arrived in Kevin and Sarah's street.

The first thing he saw was *his* car parked outside of their house. He cruised by and noticed Mary's car in the driveway. The house looked quiet, he hoped to Hell he wasn't too late.

Bruce parked in front of a nearby house and exited the car, returning the gun to the back of his waistband. He quickly padded to the front door, mindful of any stones on his bare feet. Grasping the doorknob and twisting, his shoulders slumped as he realised it was locked.

Back door. Key's under the pot plant if I need it.

Bruce raced to the side fence, vaulted over and dropped into Kevin and Sarah's backyard. He expected to be either barked at or jumped on by their loyal, but friendly Labrador, Milly. Then Bruce saw why. Milly lay in the middle of the grassed area behind the garage. Her eyes stared off to where all good dogs go when they die. Several flies were feasting off the tears of pain that had accompanied her demise. Several more had their heads buried in the large stab wound in her neck.

Bruce choked back his disgust, not just at the sight of the dead dog, but at the thought that this represented his unconscious self, the evil that dwelt within him.

What it did give him was an appreciation of what he was up against. His own pure evil self. And that meant nothing was sacred, everything may happen. Neither he nor Mary were safe.

Bruce crept across to the back door, reached out a hand and opened it enough to put an ear to the gap. There was a dull hum of voices. From the direction of the sound, he realised they were coming from the bedrooms upstairs.

Sliding the door open further, he remembered the noise it made when opened quickly. He'd told Kevin the runners needed replacing but had given up after the fifth time.

Bruce stepped inside and left the door open. He crept across the linoleum floor, pulling the gun from his waistband and flipping the safety off as he stepped into the carpeted hallway and moved up the staircase.

As he climbed, the voices grew louder, and he could make out the conversation.

"Leave her alone. You've done enough, you bastard."

Mary.

Another barely audible female voice piped up.

"Kill me. Just kill me now."

177

The voice sounded wet as if the person was talking with a mouth full of water.

"You heard the lady. She wants this."

Bruce was astonished. It was his voice.

Bed springs rang. Something thudded. Someone coughed then groaned. Mary screamed and shouted.

"No. No. No. How could I have been so wrong about you? You bastard. I wish you were dead."

Bruce sprang into action. Holding the gun straight out, he ran down towards the master bedroom and burst into the room to a nightmare beyond his imagination.

His mind reeled at the sight and tried to process it all.

The first sight was Sarah. Crucified to the wall above the bed. Her arms held in place by long knives driven through her wrists. Her feet were bound and nailed into place in much the same way. Cuts and stab wounds littered her body. Blood seeped out and ran down in crimson rivulets.

A final knife had been driven into her chest up to the handle.

"Bruce?"

Bruce's face snapped around towards Mary. She stood in front of the curtained windows to the side of the bed. Her hands were bound in front with duct tape. Her eyes wide as she regarded him.

"But? But?" she said.

Behind her, smiling like a maniac, Bruce's doppelganger held a long-bladed knife to her throat.

Bruce brought the gun up and aimed it at his double.

"Bruce, Bruce, Bruce, you've never been that good a shot. Do you think you'd hit me instead of the love of your life? I think not," said Tyr.

Bruce lowered the gun and said, "Isn't that what you want? Isn't that why you're here?"

Tyr feigned innocence. "Bruce, this isn't about Mary, all this has been about you. Don't you know what hell it's been living in that boy scout head of yours for all these years? My God you are so self-righteous, so kind, so generous, if I'd had a stomach I would have spent every moment puking." He brought the knife closer to Mary's neck. She gasped. "I just want to be rid of you forever. You're a stain on my soul that needs to be cleansed."

"You don't have a soul. You don't even have a heart. You are everything wrong with the world, everything that was wrong with me made flesh."

Tyr smiled. "Yes, now you get it. Beautiful, isn't it?"

The two stood staring intently at each other; twin sets of eyes filled with hatred for the other being.

Mary, still confused, blurted out a question. "Bruce? I don't understand. How can you be there and here?"

Tyr leaned forward and whispered into Mary's ear, "I told you I wasn't Bruce, but as usual you wouldn't believe anything he said. He's the good guy. Me, I'm his bad twin made real."

The last statement was punctuated with Tyr pointing the knife towards Bruce. A mistake.

Mary snapped her head back with as much power as she could, driving her skull into Tyr's face. The force of the blow drove Tyr's head into the glass behind.

Mary dove to the floor and shouted at Bruce. "Now. Shoot him!" she said.

Bruce brought the gun up, just as Tyr recovered and threw the knife. Bruce ducked sideways to avoid the blade, the gun fired wildly, the bullet smacking into the ceiling.

Tyr launched himself forward, tackling Bruce, and they both fell to the floor. The gun was knocked from Bruce's hand and bounced across the carpet.

Mary dove for the gun, picking it in her bound hands and turning towards the fighting pair.

Bruce uncoupled himself from Tyr and let fly with a punch that sent his twin rolling onto his back. Bruce grabbed his hand and grimaced as pain lanced up his arm.

Tyr stood unsteadily and shaped up in front of Bruce. He felt his jaw, spat blood onto the carpet and smiled. "Nice hit, boy scout."

"Fuck you."

Tyr burst out laughing. "That would be an interesting experience wouldn't it?"

Bruce realised what he meant and grimaced at the thought. He balled his fist and launched at Tyr once more, landing several punches. Tyr punched Bruce across the jaw, almost unsettling him before Bruce grabbed at Tyr's shirt, twisted and threw him onto the bed. The shirt tore free and dropped to the floor.

Tyr slammed into Sarah's feet and groaned as a knife handle stuck him in the ribs. He pulled it free and quickly threw it at Bruce. Too slow, Bruce felt the blade bury itself in his arm.

He wrenched it out, unleashing a torrent of blood, and threw the knife away, grabbing at his arm to staunch the flow, but noticing a similar wound open up on Tyr's arm.

Tyr examined the wound and grinned, before launching himself towards Bruce again.

A gunshot rang out, the bullet smacking into the wall where Tyr had been a second before. Both men turned towards Mary holding the smoking gun.

Before Bruce could react, Tyr punched at the laceration in his own arm. Bruce howled in pain. Tyr stepped sideways and landed several more punches into Bruce's face. Pain and exhaustion wracked Bruce's brain. He tried to focus but his vision clouded as the agony built.

He squared up his doppelganger and charged, tackling Tyr around the midriff and pushing them both towards the windows at the foot of the bed. The glass cracked as Bruce forced Tyr into the middle of the frame.

Tyr steadied himself and brought his fist up into Bruce's stomach, knocking the wind out of him. He launched several more punches into Bruce's midriff, pounding on top of the previous target.

Mary raised the gun and aimed at Bruce and his look-alike.

Which one is Bruce?

Each was dressed the same. Blue jeans, black belt, no t-shirt, no shoes. Each had a bleeding wound in their left arm. She couldn't tell them apart.

Finally, the pair lashed out with drunk-like punches and drew apart, panting.

Mary saw it.

The hands. The bandaged hands.

She aimed the gun and squeezed the trigger.

The noise was deafening.

The bullet hit one of the two in the centre of the chest. They grabbed at the entry wound and stumbled backwards into the window. The glass cracked and shattered with their weight. The bleeding figure disappeared through the window. The curtains ripped from the rail and followed them down. A short sharp cry was followed momentarily by a thud as the body hit the ground.

Mary leaned out and aimed the gun at the body lying on the grass below. Blood poured from the chest wound. Tyr wasn't moving, it was over. She watched for a moment just to be sure. Nothing. A small smile crossed her mouth.

A groan from behind snatched Mary's attention. She turned and dropped to one knee next to Bruce. He knelt on the ground, doubled over in pain.

"Bruce? I did it. He's gone," she said.

Bruce simply groaned even louder.

"What's wrong?"

Bruce fell forward, crashing to the floor and rolling onto his back. His hands fell away from his chest, revealing a gaping, raw wound. Blood poured from the hole. An unearthly sucking noise punctuated every part of Bruce's laboured breathing.

Mary slid a hand under his shoulder and lifted him up. She threw her other arm around and hugged him close to her. "Don't give up. Don't give up. I need you," she said.

His body was wracked with coughing, a line of blood-flecked drool ran from the corner of his mouth as he finally managed to speak.

"I'm so sorry," was all he got out before another coughing fit gripped him. He gagged several times, trying to get out more words but only coughed up a mouthful of blood. Finally, his head fell sideways, and his chest relaxed, to breath no more.

Mary screamed as she hugged her dead husband to her. "No. No. No!"

Captain Nash surveyed the scene before him.

Four ambulances were parked on the front lawn, their circling lights washing the area with red. Several squad cars were parked along the street, their lights casting red and blue across the area. Another white station wagon was parked in the driveway, the city's seal on the side with *City Coroner* emblazoned beneath.

A blonde-haired woman was under the care of two paramedics by the nearest ambulance. He recognised her as Mary McKinley, Bruce's wife and the only survivor of this fiasco.

He started to move towards her when a uniformed constable approached him.

"Sir?" he said.

Nash turned at the voice. "What is it Collins?"

"They want to bring the bodies out. Did you want to look at the scene before they do?"

"Might be a good idea. This is totally fucked up. I want to get it clear in my head what the hell happened here?" Nash noticed a uniformed constable bending over and heaving into the garden bed at the side of the house.

"Who the hell is that?"

"Fraser. First day on the job, poor bastard."

Nash grimaced and looked around to see if any of the neighbours were watching. "Get him to move around back, at least, will you?"

"He was out back, trying to compose himself, then he saw the dog. That's why he's here." Collins said.

"Dog?" asked Nash, then shook his head and went inside.

Upstairs officers, the Coroner and his men all bustled around sealing up evidence and taking photographs.

Nash peered inside the bedroom and saw Sarah's body. "Good Lord, that's Dubrough's wife?" he said to no one in particular.

The Coroner looked around and nodded.

Nash couldn't drag his eyes away from the corpse. "Finish up and get that poor woman down."

He turned and saw Bruce lying on the floor beneath the open window. His eyes stared up into Nash's own.

Nash had always thought Bruce was a good cop, but a strange one. Always on edge, always one step away from playing out something like this. Nash was wrong. Even when all the evidence pointed towards Bruce, he stayed true and died at the hands of the real culprit.

Nash had seen enough here and turned away.

Outside in the backyard, Tyr's body still lay partially wrapped in the curtain. Nash stood amazed at the uncanny likeness to Bruce's body upstairs. "This is impossible."

Collins standing next to him replied. "We've got nothing on him. He was carrying Bruce's wallet, keys and phone. If we didn't have the wife's statement, we would have guessed this was Bruce and the other one was . . . someone else."

"We won't know until the Coroner does a DNA test. Probably end up as something stupid like a long-lost twin brother," Nash said as he mopped his brow with a handkerchief and glanced up at the broken window.

At that moment, two men in dark suits approached Nash. He looked at the two detectives. "Good of you to join us."

Both of them stared at the broken corpse lying at their feet. The first detective spoke up. "Isn't that McKinley?"

Nash stared at him for a moment. "You'd think. Until you go up to the bedroom," he said.

Both detectives stared back in confusion.

"What?" the second said.

"Coroner's up there. There's a second body, looks just like this one. The rest . . . well, you're both detectives, you work it out. I've got a young woman, that's just lost her husband, to console."

The two detectives looked at Collins for an explanation.

He simply shrugged. "This is all above my pay scale," he said and walked off leaving the two of them as confused as ever.

STEPHEN HERCZEG

About the Author:

Stephen is an IT Geek, writer, actor, film maker and Taekwondo Black Belt based in Canberra Australia. He has been writing for over twenty years and has completed a couple of dodgy novels, sixteen feature length screenplays and dozens of short stories and scripts.

Stephen's scripts TITAN, Dark are the Woods, Control *and* Death Spores *have found success in international screenwriting competitions with a win, two runner-up and two top ten finishes.*
His horror stories have featured in various anthologies including: Sproutlings; Hells Bells; Trickster's Treats #1, #2 and #3; Shades of Santa; Below the Stairs; Behind the Mask; Beyond the Infinite; Beside the Seaside; The Body Horror Book; Anemone Enemy; Petrified Punks; Beginnings; Sea of Secrets, Demonic Carnival; Deep Space; A Tribute to H.G. Wells; What If?; Through Death's Door *and* Coffins and Dragons.

Over forty of his drabbles have been accepted by Blood Song Books; Black Hare Press; Fantasia Divinity and ThingsInTheWell.

Several of his Sherlock Holmes pastiches have been accepted for inclusion in anthologies published by Belanger Books and MX Publishing.

You can catch Stephen at his Facebook page:
https://www.facebook.com/stephenherczegauthor

THIS IS THE DAWNING
(PART VI)

Helena McAuley

Dawnesque sunlight filtered through the curtains and brought me to wakefulness, like the gentle caress of a lover's hand. I awoke with a smile. Good morning, sunlight! Good morning, world! How lovely to be here today. I stretched languidly before I turned to the Bakelite clock beside my bed. 2:00pm. Good. Time to get up.

The oats and corn kernels I'd left soaking overnight were ready, the brine having revived them to a fat, plump state. I nodded in satisfaction, then took the liver out of the fridge to fry it; only lightly. No need to turn it to cinders. The window of my bedsit opened on to the roof of the butchers shop below, a great place to get cheap liver. Across the very busy road was a very busy train station that seemed to run all hours of the day or night.

Carefully, I climbed out onto the butcher's roof, set down the plate of liver, and pulled my shawl around my shoulders.

"Puss, puss, puss, puss, *puuuusss!*" I squealed into the blazing afternoon air, still cool and dark in the shadow of my southerly facing flat. The pretty kitties heard my call and came running up for their breakfast.

I want to make it very clear that I have never kept pets. But I have had a lot of companions in my time. *Familiars*, I believe the term once was. Animals with which you share your home, your food, your life, but whom are never under your control.

"Here, Darryl. Here, Shirley. Here, Kevin," I cooed and they began to devour. Hmm . . . That's odd . . . I counted again, to be sure the old eyes weren't playing tricks with me. "Where's Tracey?"

When the cats were replete with food, sunning themselves at the furthest point of the roof, licking liver fat from their paws, I ducked back through the window and drained the oats and corn. In great handfuls I scattered it across the roof and sat to wait for the birds to flock in. Pigeons, sparrows, and even the occasional seagull greeted me. The cats watched them with lazy curiosity, but their stomachs were too full to be bothered to hunt. Once I was satisfied that everyone would play nice, I climbed back through the window and wandered downstairs.

It was easy to enjoy the hustle and bustle of the shopping strip below. There were people everywhere—going to the greengrocer, standing in line for takeaway coffee, getting a late lunch at the Thai restaurant—but I could move among them unnoticed, even when manifest. I don't unmanifest often, don't rebuke any of the restrictions of a human form like my fellows do. Why bother? We incarnate as *humans*, why not experience a *human* life? Why would you separate yourself from so much joy?

This has been my human form for sixty-three years, and I have loved every moment of it. Unlike any other of the Twelve, I do not need to incarnate. When they decide to descend to the material realm and become encased in a physical body they enter into slumber. Incarnation begins with a long, slow process of awakening; sometimes this can take years, but more often it takes decades. Perhaps it begins a drop at a time; a memory here, a splash of knowledge there, until they have finally woken enough to incarnate. But there are times when it happens in an instant; triggered by threat, by shock, or by *need*. I feel for my fellows, I really do. The process of incarnation looks incredibly painful, and if they are open to me whilst they incarnate I can feel the rending of their being as they twist and tear and are reformed, remembering *who they are*. But I've never experienced it myself.

I am always born full in the knowledge that *I am* the spirit of Gemini. I remember my home amongst the stars, and I remember my previous incarnations, my skills and abilities, how my body is distinctly *not human* and utterly subject to my will. I always remember who I have been. Conversely, I simply need to discover who I am now. I usually develop a sense of self about three years of age—my goodness! What a time of immense *joy* that is! If I so desired, I could halt my physical and mental growth right there and remain a three-year-old forever!

Oh. What an intriguing thought . . . Maybe I'll try that with my next incarnation. But, then again, being three years old forever may prove most difficult, as well as highly conspicuous . . .

But, usually, I allow myself to age with the passing of the years, just as humans do. I allow my physical body to remain subject to the material realm, just as humans do. I eat, sleep, get sick, and wither, just as humans do. And what *fun* it is! Then, once I have allowed this body to pass, I take time to rest among the stars, and revel in my mind becoming one with the universe, watching the Earth unfold in its own journey before the excitement builds to a crescendo and I can no longer hold myself back from joining in that celebration of *life*.

It's a pity my fellows do not experience incarnation as I do. Their lives would be so much simpler if they only learnt to let go.

And so I walked along the streets, breathing the sweet air tinged with flowers and fumes and listening to the song of the day, and feeling the result of sixty-three years of a human existence. There is the bad hip I acquired from dancing on a rickety coffee table, and the osteoarthritis that time has gifted me, the bunions from a childhood of ill-fitting shoes, and the old-age blood-disorder from a genetically predisposed pancreas, as well as the faulty liver from an overindulgence in sherry. I see the doctors and accept treatment enough to keep the body functioning, and to keep my pension, though I am not above using the ability to *command* humans in order to have doctors sign those highly unnecessary forms. I don't do it too much. The lovely young GP at my review last month looked over my file with a near horrified expression on her face.

"Aren't you in an awful lot of pain?" she had asked.

"Oh, yes!" I had replied. "It's *exquisite!*"

She hadn't been quite sure how to take that one.

I hadn't bothered to keep track of time whilst I wandered the streets, but I hadn't strayed too far from home when I found what I was looking for. A mange-ridden little tabby, stiff and still in the gutter.

"Oh, Tracey," I lamented as I bent down to stroke her fur one last time, even though it was crusty with dry blood and swarming with flies. "Oh, poor little kitty."

There was a moment of deep sorrow and regret, and tears welled in my eyes. I must have been a sight—an old woman in her bedraggled clothes clutching her shawl about her and weeping in the street over a dead stray. But the mourning passed, as it always does, and I smiled down at her broken little body.

"Sleep well, my pretty kitty," I bade her. "I'll see you when I return to the stars."

I hobbled back to my tiny flat, again fully able to enjoy the breadth of the day. An idea suddenly occurred to me.

Capricorn! Oh, dear, Capricorn! I called out to him.

There was the feeling of mild irritation, like a repressed groan. *What do* you *want?*

191

Come and have a cup of tea.

You know I don't drink tea, he replied.

You drink my *tea,* I reminded him. *But you're in luck, because I also have sherry.*

There was a pause filled with a disquieted tremor; an old man spluttering curses, I imagine. It brought a smile to my lips.

Fine, he acquiesced. *I'll be there soon.*

I stopped at the grocer on the way home and bought a couple of handfuls of walnuts so we'd have something to nosh with our sherry—well, so *I* would have something, Capricorn rarely indulges in foodstuffs. I've never seen one so uptight in all my incarnations; human or not. Oh, yes, he's a right prickly fellow, but his heart is in the right place. Some others of the Twelve would add that his heart is in *just the right place* for a dagger to be plunged into it. But not I; I would not be so base. Though his relationships with the others is somewhat worrisome to me, Capricorn will have quite the role to play, and sooner than he thinks. Every chicken he has ever sent into the world will be coming home to roost.

I hoped he had not destroyed the hutch. At least not too badly.

The bad hip only allowed me to take the stairs one at a time, and the arthritis meant it took me a full thirty seconds to insert the key to the door and manage grip enough to turn it. By the time I managed to close the door behind me he was already there, rummaging through my CD collection; Carole King, Joni Mitchell, and, of course, *ahhh . . . John Denver!*

"Excellent idea, Capricorn," I said to him by way of greeting. "Some music to suit the mood!" I poured the walnuts into a bowl on the kitchen table and took the CD from his hand, my other arm curling to embrace him as I did.

"Away from me, wench," he muttered as he shrugged off my arm. It's this little game we play; I lavish him with affection, and he rebukes me at every turn. It entertains me to watch him squirm, though I wonder why he bothers with the front. I know I'm his favourite.

With Mr Denver graciously singing the words of my soul, I returned to the kitchen cupboards and took two glasses for the sherry—making sure Capricorn's glass was *extra* full. He stood awkwardly in front of the stereo when I passed him the glass, and he took a generous sip as I installed myself on the wicker couch.

"What do you want, Gemini?"

"I spoke with Pisces last night," I began. "She's worried about you."

He moved to set the glass down, but it did not quite leave his hand. "She's been worried about me for the last three decades," he mutters. "What about this time?"

"Well . . ." I stretched languidly and then curled my legs under me on the couch ". . . she's found out you've given up your home, your possessions, any *human* contacts. And she's worried about you."

Again, the move to release the glass, and, again, the failure to do so. "I have not had an abode for years," he said to me. "Why would she be concerned about this now?"

I smiled, in a way I know infuriates him. "Because I only told her last night."

His body stilled, and I saw a range of emotions flash through his eyes. Disbelief, irritation, anger, and finally a kind of acceptance. He shook his head and lifted the glass to his lips again. "Meddlesome, two-faced bitch," he muttered before he took a sip.

A peal of joyous laugher escaped me. I muffled it with a sip of sherry, but even with a full sip burning on my tongue I could not completely extinguish the chortles.

"How *is* your relationship with Pisces these days?" I asked him.

He shrugged, and finally acquiesced to take a seat. "It's fine," he told me. "We speak every so often."

"And Leo?"

"We haven't spoken in some time, but I keep tabs," he said with an air of indifference. "He's doing quite well for himself, as usual."

"What about Libra?"

Now he gave pause, the glass still poised on his lips, but his eyes slowly shifted towards me. He swallowed and lowered the glass to his lap. "Are you going to ask me about everyone?"

I smiled. No, no, not 'smiled'; I *grinned.* Dear Capricorn, your shrewdness verges on paranoia. Or should it be that your paranoia verges on shrewdness? I can never tell.

"Found me out so quickly?" I asked with feigned disappointment. "Darn. I so hoped I could squeeze a little more gossip out of you before you caught on."

He set the glass on the table with a tight jaw and a restrained growl. "Goodbye, Gemini." Without a backwards glance he headed for the door.

"Someone is looking for me," I told him.

He paused with his hand on the door handle. Ah, *intrigue.* That old carrot. I knew I could get him to stay. Another irate puff escaped him as he shut the door and turned back.

"Who?"

I indicated the chair and the sherry with a wave of my hand. There was only a moment of internal conflict before he sullenly took the chair and retrieved the glass, throwing it back in one mouthful and helping himself to more.

"Who is looking for you, Gemini?"

I said the name in a conspiratorial whisper, "*Sagittarius.*"

He watched me, waiting for me to say more. It's delicious how I can wrap him around my finger like this. Dance him like a marionette, the strings belonging only to me. None other of the Twelve can control Capricorn like this—only me. It's another of the little games we play; he thinks he has autonomy, and I only make him dance a little, so that afterwards he is left with *just* enough suspicion to wonder at how much I have played him. Don't misunderstand me, I love him dearly, and everything I do to him, I do for love *of* him. Or for my own enjoyment. There is a reason he calls me the Two-Faced Bitch, after all.

"I understand she's the only one you've not been able to locate," I said.

"The only one who is *incarnate*," he corrected me. "Taurus escaped me until recently, Aries may not have taken human form, and Aquarius is not yet incarnate. But, no," he admitted, "I haven't found Sagittarius, yet. Not this incarnation, at least."

"She's hiding from you for a reason," I said, again at the volume of a whisper.

His eyes did not leave mine. "She's detracting from the order."

I merely touched my finger to my nose.

He stood again, spitting half-finished curses this time. "Damn her. She's been a malcontent for millennia. Each Dawning she's tried to pull others away from consensus."

"And the Dawning is upon us."

He stopped in his pacing. "I know," he finally said.

"The last one before the Age of Aquarius, and the fulfilment of your plan."

A look of grim apprehension tightened his features. Does he show this vulnerability to any but me? In my heart of hearts, I hope not. *This* Capricorn I have known through all of my incarnations of this Age. He has chosen not to dis-incarnate, and it has given me a chance for continuity that I have not had with any other of our fellows. I know myself at the moment of my birth, and *he* knows *me*, also. All others have changed and fallen away, but he has always sought me out, and each time I have embraced him as kin. The others may become consumed with the costume they don for each incarnation, but Capricorn's steadfast insecurity and obsession with his *plan* has led him to remain within the one mask. A mask that has adhered itself to him like a second skin, has melded with his very being, until it replaced his true face. I know it is slowly tearing him apart, unravelling him like so much unwanted string, but his consistency has given me comfort over the centuries. He is *mine*; at times my puppet on a string, at times my doll to entertain myself, and at times my one true friend, but *mine* nonetheless.

"This is her last gambit," I reminded him. "Perhaps it will make her desperate."

The strain on his face was only superseded by the anxiety and fear in his eyes. "What does she want with you?"

I could almost believe his worry was for me. Almost.

I shrugged my shoulders, leaving behind the melodrama and conspiracy. "I don't know. Perhaps she simply wants some of my fabulous sherry."

"Please, Gemini," he pleaded, exposed and contrite. "You see the Other Side. What should I *do?*"

That beautiful vulnerability. Reserved only for *me*.

I smiled my most beneficent smile. "Follow your heart," I told him. "It will lead you to the right place."

I think he very nearly believed me.

We drank and spoke into the night, but there was nothing of further consequence in our discussion. Always the prig, Capricorn forced his human body to dispel the alcohol before he unmanifest and bid me farewell. I finished the bottle of sherry and the walnuts he'd left untouched, before preparing tomorrow's liver for my pretty kitties and leaving it out for them early. The birds would fend for themselves, I knew, but the cats had habituated to my daily custom. I took my shawl and set out into the night.

It was so late in the night as to be early morning. The Witching Hour. I love this time of night; past the time when even the midnight-oil burners had taken to their beds, but not yet early enough for the worm-catchers to rise. The world was calm and still, each gentle noise enough to break through the wall of still air and shatter it. My footsteps cracked like the strides of a thunder god as I passed out of the streets and into the alleyways, each hum and tremor from my lips as omnipresent as the hymn of an angel. There was a dampness to the air that strained to settle and subjugate the streets, but I thwarted it with every step until it bent to my will and became a gentle breeze.

The overpass was the most subdued of them all. Here even the wind refused to visit. The echo of the cars below was an intermittent roar that split the night. But that, too, would pass, and solemnity would again gently assert itself.

THIS IS THE DAWNING (PART VI)

I raised myself onto the balustrade, humming quietly and swinging my feet, merely enjoying the night. The absence of streetlights cast shadows about me that even the moon could not break, but this only afforded me a grander view of the stars. I took in their beauty as I waited.

I did not have to wait long.

I did not see her manifest, but I doubt she took the trouble of walking all the way here. At first she was nothing but a silhouette, but soon her form asserted itself—a goddess deigned to prescribe herself a human form. She was always so fond of making herself the pretty one.

She approached me and I smiled. Her own visage was bleak.

My smile deepened. "Sagittarius."

Ten minutes later my body struck the asphalt below, splitting my skull and shattering my bones. Don't weep for me, my death was a quick one. Immediate, in fact. And despite the rift that tore it in two, my smile never left my face.

Capricorn had better work hard. Sagittarius is not toying with dissention, this time.

This, my dearest friends, is how wars begin. One tiny act of insurrection at a time.

To be continued in the next edition of the Zodiac Series—

Cancer . . .

About the Author:

Helena McAuley has studied for years to become a polyglot. However, she is terrible at languages, and if her writing is anything to go by, she has yet to master even one.

Despite this, Helena is still able to say "Cheers" in twelve different languages, including Welsh and Romanian. Do NOT get her drunk and try to cheers her, you will be there all night.

'This is the Dawning' is a serialised debut that will be published throughout the ASF Zodiac series. So if you want to see where Capricorn's heart leads him and Doug, you'd better keep reading.

She can be found twit-ing, insta-ing, and occasionally facebooked under the handle @thathmc

(The author usually tries to end her bio with something funny relating to the zodiacal symbol for the anthology. However, she can't think of anything, so instead she would like to say Happy Birthday to a special someone. They know who they are.)

ABOUT AUSSIE SPECULATIVE FICTION

Aussie Speculative Fiction is a recently established group
which was created to support and promote Australian
speculative fiction writers.

Check out our links:

www.facebook.com/Aussiespeculativefiction/

www.twitter.com/aussiefiction

www.aussiespeculativefiction.com

www.books2read.com/rl/asf

ABOUT DEADSET PRESS

Deadset Press is the publishing imprint of Aussie Speculative Fiction—a community aimed at supporting Australian and Kiwi authors. You can learn more at:

www.aussiespeculativefiction.com

ALSO BY DEADSET PRESS

www.ingramcontent.com/pod-product-compliance
Lightning Source LLC
Chambersburg PA
CBHW020144120726
47903CB00007B/2400